"Are you really the one they call Longarm?"

"I fear I must be since I ain't met anyone else called that in recent memory. Is my Nadene brother asking friendly, or am I glad as hell I brought my gun along this evening?"

The pack leader laughed and said, "You have spoken to Nadene before, I can see. I am sorry you were not here the last time we took the warpath. It would have been a good fight. I am called Wolverines Fear His Smell. You can call me Big Stink. I am not at war with your kind this summer. You did not take advantage of my drunken brother, even though you have a gun and they would not hang you for using it on one of us. I think I will let you live, Longarm."

"You think you got much choice, Big Stink?"

TABOR EVANS

LONGARM

AND THE
INLAND PASSAGE

A JOVE BOOK

LONGARM AND THE INLAND PASSAGE

A Jove Book/published by arrangement with
the author

PRINTING HISTORY
Jove edition/May 1986

ISBN: 0-515-08569-3

Jove Books are published by The Berkley Publishing Group,
200 Madison Avenue, New York, N.Y. 10016.
The words "A JOVE BOOK" and the "J" with sunburst
are trademarks belonging to Jove Publications, Inc.

PRINTED IN THE UNITED STATES OF AMERICA

LONGARM

AND THE
INLAND PASSAGE

Chapter 1

Longarm lay awake in bed a spell wondering why. The battered brass alarm clock he'd set for six had neither gone off nor died in its sleep. He could still hear it ticking. But there surely was a lot of daylight glaring in at him if it wasn't time to get up yet.

Then Longarm figured out where he was and rolled over with a sheepish grin. For once he didn't have to worry about resetting the clock and waking up for sure by eight or so. For once he wasn't going to show up for work out of breath and have that tattle-tale office clock on Marshal Billy Vail's wall pointing its fingers at a good old boy who meant well. For once he got to sleep as late as he wanted on a working day. For he was in the sack in a stateroom of the steamship *Sitka Sally*, steaming somewhere in the Inland Passage running north to Seward's Folly or, to put it more politely, the recently American territory of Unalaska, Alaska, or whatever the hell they aimed to call it, once they made their minds up.

He lay on his side, trying to go back to sleep, for at least two minutes, or the time it takes a gent to discover he just can't do it. He was hungry and thirsty as well. So he swore, tossed the bedclothes off, and got up. It was just as well he did so alone in the tiny stateroom. Even friends who admired the way Longarm looked stark naked had been known to gasp when the big deputy marshal got up. Longarm moved suddenly for a man his size and tended to loom in such a small room.

There was a bitty tin sink built into the bulkhead. He turned the brass tap, ran a tumbler of water, and spat it out with a curse when he tasted it. But salt water was good enough to wash and shave with, albeit a mite cold to his fancy. They had told him icebergs came bobbing down the Inland Passage even in high summer. He nicked himself shaving. That was hard to do when a man kept his razor well stropped and knew how to handle it, but goosebumps were easy to cut off by accident.

He saw now why so many of the crew aboard this vessel sported full beards. He was glad he didn't have to shave his upper lip, even if that gal in Seattle had complained his heavy moustache tickled.

He got dressed to go aft to the main salon and get some food and drink. He was glad now that they had made him wear his sissy tobacco tweed suit and vest on this mission. Back in Denver it could hurt like hell on a hot day to wear wool. But the morning air up Alaska way was cold and clammy, even inside a steamship.

He found the main salon almost deserted, early as it was. A Chinese barkeep was polishing glasses behind the mahogany. A woman in a big veiled hat was sitting in a far corner, writing something at one of the bitty desks along that wall. Longarm ordered a schooner of beer at the bar and asked how one could get steak and eggs around here.

The Chinese man poured him a pint of Anchor Beer with no argument, but said the kitchen wasn't ready to serve breakfast yet.

So the tall and now morose lawman carried the schooner over to one of the writing tables, sat down, and lit a three-for-a-nickel cheroot. The beer tasted refreshing, too. They had told him before it came all the way up from Frisco in glass-lined, not tar-lined kegs.

The steamship line provided free writing materials, as well they should, considering the price they charged for second-class passage. Longarm had asked them to sell him a third-class ticket and the rascals had said there was neither a first- or third-class passage aboard this generally second-class tub.

There was an inkwell on the table, but Longarm used his own stub pencil as he proceeded to do some homework on a sheet of free stationery. The map said it was nine hundred and thirty miles from Seattle to Sitka and the Justice Department said Longarm could charge Uncle Sam six cents a mile for travel expenses in the field. He was sure some smart ass who'd been teacher's pet had settled on that figure just to make it tough on boys who'd had their schooling cut short by the war. Anyone with a lick of sense knew U. S. money was based on the decimal system. So why in thunder did a man have to multiply by damn fool half-dozens?

Longarm never forgot his manners entirely if there was a woman anywhere nearby, but he was muttering as he tried to figure out just how much he was losing on this infernal voyage. Down in the States a deputy in the field tended to come out ahead on his expense account, since few horses charged six cents a mile to be ridden. The infernal boat fare didn't break down to even-cents a mile at all.

"May I be of some service, monsieur?" asked a friendly female voice like an angel from above. Longarm slid off the chair, took off his Stetson and, sure enough, it was the gal with the big veiled hat. At this range he could see she had no reason on earth to cover her face with black mesh. She said, "I could not help but notice, as I was about to return to my own room, monsieur seems to be trying to work out a mathamatical problem and, forgive me, monsieur has one decimal point in the wrong place if he is trying to multiply 930 by 6. Would you like me to try?"

He said he surely would and added as he seated her, "You don't talk like a usual schoolmarm, ma'am."

She dimpled under her veil. "Thank you for not remarking on my English. I fear I would have a time indeed teaching school in your country. *Mais* numbers speak the same language all over the world, *non?*"

She picked up the pencil stub, rewrote his problem on a fresh sheet, then asked politely what they were trying to figure out. When he told her she laughed and said, *Mais* that is so simple. I, too, am traveling on a limited budget. So I already know this *très* ordinary vessel is charging us a fraction less than one of your American nickels a mile, so . . ."

"Right. I'll wind up in Sitka ten or twelve dollars richer than when I got on," he cut in, adding with a sigh, "That ain't much, but it would have hurt worse the other way. Would you be offended if I bought you a drink now

4

that I'm so rich, ma'am?"

She trilled more than she exactly laughed and then she said, "Only on condition you allow me to buy the second round. I am the Princess Natasha Baranov. My friends call me Tasha, and *your* friends, monsieur . . . ?"

"Oh, I'm Deputy U. S. Marshal Custis Long, and my friends call me just plain Custis. It ain't my fault. My folks picked it out."

She blinked under her veil. *"Mon Dieu,* I just read about you in the Seattle papers! Are not you the famous Marshal Longarm, Custis?"

He shrugged and replied, "I'm trying not to be so famous and I'm only a deputy, not a full marshal. What do you drink, Tasha?"

She said they didn't have her brand aboard this *très fatigué* steamer but that she would settle for gin and tonic. She stayed in the bentwood chair he'd given up while he brought her drink back from the bar. He hauled another chair from another writing table and sat as they clinked glasses.

She was just drinking politely, he could see, when she put her glass down and got her veil out of the way by unpinning her big hat and putting it on another table. Her black hair stayed pinned up, of course, but he could tell it came down below her waist at bedtime and had to remind himself it was nowhere near late enough to consider that notion, pretty as she was. Her heart-shaped face read about thirty, give or take some sadness. Her big dark eyes were sad, too, even though she smiled too much, as gals tended to when they weren't sure of a gent one way or the other.

To keep from talking too much himself, Longarm stared past her through the side glass of the salon. The shoreline they were passing at the moment was pretty, but after passing one spruce-covered mountain after another the novelty sure wore thin. Half to himself, Longarm said, "They say we ought to be getting into Sitka before three, Lord willing and the creeks don't rise."

She looked sincerely puzzled. "Don't try to figure out my West-By-God-Virginia sayings, Tasha. Sometimes I don't know just what they mean myself," he told her.

"Do you have friends to meet you when we dock at Sitka, Custis?"

"Not hardly. Do you?"

She sighed and replied, "Not any more. You Americans bought Alaska from the Tsar when I was still a little girl. I was, as you may have guess from my French accent, raised and educated after that in Petrograd. I mean the Petrograd in Russia, not the silly little Alaskan fishing village of the same name."

Longarm nodded sagely, wondering if he was supposed to say something. He had met Russian aristocrats before, so he wasn't surprised to hear they all spoke French instead of Russian. He had already figured out she was around thirty and that added up, since Seward had bought the old Russian colony almost a generation back, even if nobody in Washington knew what to do with it as yet. A thirty-year-old gal would have been a teen-ager, not a little girl, when her Tsar sold the rug out from under her in the Sixties. But a lady had the constitutional right to fib some about her age.

As he was counting in his head Tasha was asking him why he'd been sent to Sitka. He had to calculate fast in a different direction, before he decided there was no need to lie when the truth was in his favor and would be all over town in no time in any case. He said, "They sent

6

me up from the States to identify a prisoner the U. S. Navy wants identified quickly. If he's who they think he is he faces a court-martial for desertion. If he's who he says he is, he doesn't, since the Navy would never enlist such a rascal."

"I'm afraid my English is not up to understanding that, Custis."

He shook his head. "You ain't confused. I ain't confused. The Navy's confused. As of up to now, no regular civilian government's been set up for the Alaska Territory. So the U. S. Navy gets to run everything from its naval base at the old Russian capital at Sitka. As you might imagine, the officers running the Navy Shore Patrol ain't as smart about outlaws as us Justice Department agents, but they try. A week or more back, a whaler had to put in unexpectedly at Sitka when it hit unexpected ice and sprung a leak. The Navy sent some gents aboard to look over their papers and such. The first mate was either a gent who disenlisted from the U. S. Navy in the Sandwich Islands without permission, or he sure looked like him. So they have him in the Sitka brig awaiting court-martial for desertion or a sincere apology. We'll know better once I get there to look him over."

Tasha shuddered and murmured, "Oh, the poor thing. Will they shoot him or hang him if he's the man you can identify?"

Longarm chuckled. "Neither," he said. "They don't execute deserters in peacetime. Thy just make 'em *wish* they was dead for a spell at hard labor. I don't know why they give 'em dishonorable discharge papers. I've yet to see one printed on yellow paper framed on anyone's parlor wall. I'm not going there to testify against him on desertion. I ain't never been in the U. S. Navy. But I do

7

know the man the suspect's *claiming* he is, *loud."*

"Oh, then your mission is not to arrest a man but to clear his good name?"

He took a sip of Anchor, grinned crookedly, and replied, "The last thing old Soapy Smith might have is a good name. But, like I said, it seems doubtful he ever deserted any navy. Only a short while ago I ran him out of Denver with a .44-40 slug in his hide where it didn't slow him down much. I find it hard to believe, too. But once they let the suspect talk to a lawyer, the first thing he asked for, after a key to his cell, was me. He said he was sure I could identify him on sight as we had sighted down gun barrels at each other in the past, and that does leave a lasting impression."

This time it was Tasha's turn to laugh. She said, "You Americans are incredible! In my country such a simple matter would have been settled so much easier."

He nodded gravely. "I know. I met another high-toned Russian gal called Tasha one time. She told me how easy it was to get a free ride to Siberia."

He didn't add that the other Tasha went in for French loving as well as a French accent. It wouldn't have been polite, even if they'd looked at all like one another. This particular Russian hadn't even said she wanted to hold hands with him. He feared he might have insulted her Tsar with that last remark about Siberia, fair as it might be, so he said, "Well, even a rascal has some rights under our constitution and, though Soapy Smith don't deserve a kind word from a skunk, it'd still be wrong to court-martial him for a crime he hasn't had a chance to commit yet. They call him Soapy Smith because he became famous in Denver for slickering rubes with a con game too complicated to go into, but involving a cake of soap worth mayhaps one cent, sold for a silver dollar. He got so famous indeed that I just couldn't see fit to live in the same town with him, so I run him out. He didn't think I could, me being a federal lawman and him being too slick to bust federal laws. But we worked out an agreement, after I winged him a mite and asked where he'd like the next bullet. He left Denver swearing he'd do me dirt one day and danged if he hasn't. For I sure never wanted to visit Seward's Folly before they got at least one decent dance hall built. No offense, Tasha, but I hear even Sitka is a sort of primitive place, and . . . Hey, how come we're standing out to sea right now? Ain't Sitka on the Inland Passage?"

She shook her head and said, *"Mais non,* it lies at the head of Sitka Sound, on the seaward side of Baranov Island."

He frowned thoughtfully at her and asked, "Do tell? How come they named your family after an Alaskan island, Princess?"

She smiled modestly and explained, "The island was named after my family. My grandfather was officially the royal governor, of course, but we actually owned more than the island itself, despite what a few Russian serfs and those horrid Tlingits might have told you Americans."

He thought about that through another sip of Anchor. Then he nodded and said, "I suspicioned you might be bitter about something. I ain't fixing to apologize for stealing your old homestead, since I never knew until just now who was living there when your Tsar sold the land to *my* uncle without consulting me. Are you on your way back to claim at least a few acres back, Tasha?"

She sighed. "I don't know what I would do with

Tlingit-infested woodlands if I could get title to them. If you must know, I am returning to look for something a . . . well . . . dotty old aunt left behind. Forgive me, but I do not think I should tell you more until I have a better grasp of your American laws about such things."

He nodded soberly. "I ain't with the Revenue Department, but Justice is close enough to make folk thoughtful about buried treasures, ma'am. So let's say no more about it. I wonder when they figure to serve breakfast aboard this tub. If I was back in Denver at this time of day I'd have eaten already and be worried about getting to my office on time."

She stared out the side glass at the now less smooth water and said, "How odd. It does seem as if we've known one another for ages and yet, as you say, it is still early. I am not sure I shall stay for breakfast, however. Regard the whitecaps we are steaming through now."

He glanced out, shrugged, and said, "That sea don't look too rough to me, Tasha. I've rid out whiter water in a canoe and I ain't got seasick yet."

She grimaced and reached for her hat and veil. "Speak for yourself. I confess I have always been *très* sensitive to *mal de mer,* and once we round that point ahead and swing north this species of deplorable paddlewheeler is sure to roll *très formidable!*"

She looked like she was getting sick already. Longarm rose, grabbed his Stetson with one hand and her elbow with the other, and said, "I'd best show you to your stateroom, then. Next to an hour's rest under an apple tree, there ain't nothing better than lying down for seasickening." As they headed forward, he couldn't help adding, "You sure must be a princess, no offense. For this boat ain't rocking all that bad. I've had Denver rock

10

worse, after a few too many, and, shoot, I ain't even trying to balance us."

She moved closer to him, moaning, "Oh, don't let me fall! I feel so dizzy!"

He let go of her elbow and wrapped the arm about her instead. Her perfume sure smelled nice, closer up. Her hip was rubbing against his now as he walked her along the companionway, hoping her quarters were way up in the bow and glad he packed his .44 on the other hip. He still found it hard to believe a sensible-talking gal like Tasha could get seasick this easily. He had to study on it to feel the deck moving under his army boots enough to matter. But some folk found the tobacco he smoked sort of sickening, so he reckoned it took all kinds to make the world more interesting. It was too bad a gal this handsome had to get sick before a man could get so close to her, though.

They came to a door on the far side of the paddle boxes and Tasha stopped him and fished for the key in her muff-like purse. She opened up but didn't invite him in, so he said he'd best see about some ventilation and crossed over to her porthole. As he twisted the dogs he heard her pleading not to open it lest the seas come in to drown them. He laughed, then cursed one brass dog until it allowed itself to be twisted before his fingers broke or vice versa. He was too polite to say the air in her stuffy stateroom was musky and over-perfumed, so he said, "Sea air don't have the effect on one's innards that sea waves do, Tasha. You just flop down and let this cool breeze blow over you, hear? We're way too high to worry about waves."

As he turned from the open port he saw she'd shut the door and that she'd taken his suggestion about lying down and then some. She was sprawled on the bunk along one wall with her hair unbound and her bodice unbuttoned. It was a good thing her black hair was so long, considering how far down she'd unbuttoned. He gulped and said, "There you go. I'll get out of here so you can get undressed entire."

"What will I do if there's a real storm and green water does pour in on me, alas?" she pleaded.

He laughed despite himself and said, "You'll get wet. But don't fret your pretty head about green water, Princess. I may look dumb, but I'm sure I can figure out how to shut a porthole in a real storm and I'll be keeping an eye on them whitecaps for you. Try to get some sleep. That way you won't know if you're sick or not, and by the time you wake up we ought to be there."

He put his hand on the latch. She said, "Wait. There is a bottle of vodka in my trunk, under the bed. I still owe you a drink, and I certainly need a stiff one myself right now."

Longarm found a hook for his Stetson and dropped to one knee to haul the Saratoga trunk out. It wasn't locked. He wasn't sure it shouldn't have been, as he opened the lid and saw all sorts of she-male unmentionables a lady generally didn't allow a gent to look at unless she knew him mighty well. But she was moaning desperately now, so he fished through the scented silk and lace-edged notions until he found the bottle of vodka. It had been unsealed, but he could see she hadn't drunk more than a cup or so in her previous travels. He pulled the cork with his teeth and rose to look about for glasses. The steamer played a sudden trick on them by hitting a wave wrong and bucking like a big lazy bronc.

Longarm hung onto the bottle as the trunk slid under

the bunk again, slamming its own lid. Meanwhile, he landed on top of the bunk and Tasha, knocking the wind out of her and popping one of her hitherto tightly confined breasts out the front of her bodice.

He rolled his weight off her, some, and glanced down into the bottle to see if anything was swimming in the vodka and to give her time to tuck her breast away. She laughed and said, *"Merde alors,* what an approach!" Then, just as he was about to say something dumb about glasses, she sat up, wrapped her arms around him, and was kissing him French indeed.

Naturally he had to recork the bottle, if she didn't want a drink just now. So he had to reach an arm around her either way and put the cork back in behind her. He tossed the bottle aside on the bedding and, as long as his hands were back there in any case, hauled her in for a better grasp of the situation as she went on proving there were some gals in this cruel world who didn't seem to mind a moustache at all. But when he discovered yet more buttons running up the spine of her complicated dress, and idly opened one, she came up for air and gasped. "Wait. This is my best dress and I cannot get off this vessel with it missing buttons! Let *me* do it. You men can be so clumsy about such matters."

She proceeded to undress and, since he was as good a sport, they did it the first time stark and friendly. From the way she was moaning and groaning as he pounded her, he suspected that if she'd ever been seasick in the first place, this sure was the proper cure for whatever was ailing her.

He didn't ask if she felt better, once they'd broken the ice with a fast mutual orgasm and were cuddled naked atop the covers to share a smoke, catch their wind, and plan more interesting positions. He asked her how often they might be doing this once they reached Sitka and she started to cry.

He took a drag on his cheroot, patted her bare shoulder soothingly, and said, "Hell, don't blubber up on me, honey. I hardly ever fight duels over women, in case you're worried about some gent in Sitka. You told me you had nobody meeting you there, and I've never even *seen* the fool place. But if you want to make this the whole show, I promise not to cry. We don't even have to know one another once the boat docks, if that's the way you want it."

She sobbed, "That is not the way I want it, and you know it. Did you think I was faking it just now?"

"The thought never occurred to me, since up until this odd discussion I saw no reason for you to be screwing with ulterior motives. Now suppose you say what in thunder all these dramatics are about?"

She sighed and asked, "Can't you guess, darling?"

"You're confusing me," he told her. "I'm an easy-going lover and since I really like most women, as pals, I mean, I'm prepared to go along with any notions that don't wind up painful, harmful to others, or just silly. I said I don't know any other gals in Alaska. So if you want to shack up some when we get to Sitka I can't think of anyone I'd rather shack up with until it's time to leave. On the other hand, if you have your own reasons for making this a one-time delight, that's jake with me. If there was a third choice, I'd go along with it. But there ain't. We can linger a while or we can call it quits. The choice is your own to make. So why in the hell are you acting like I'm beating you up, for God's sake?"

She sighed. "God, or the Orthodox Church, has more

14

to say about the private life of a Russian princess than you may imagine. It is true I have no close relations living in Sitka now. But your silly government has allowed the Russian missionaries to stay on. Worse yet, they have allowed the Orthodox Cathedral of Saint Michael to remain open in our lost colony."

He snuffed out his smoke and said, "My government ain't silly. It's fair. If they let the Mormons have a temple in Salt Lake it only stands to reason Russians can have their own kind of church in Sitka. Are you worried about the mission reporting back to the Tsar about you and me?"

"Oh, Custis, *mon amour,* if only you knew how the Petrograd court indulges in gossip of the most vicious kind!"

He nodded. "I ain't never been to many royal courts, but I can imagine. You should have heard what the Denver society gals had to say about Miss Silverheels trying to go straight. I get the picture, now. A princess has to worry about her reputation and I ain't the sort of gent a princess is allowed to mess with."

She sobbed again. "Oh, if only you were at least a baron! We are both sophisticated travelers, so I know better than to tell you I had no idea we were going to arrive in this *très* naughty position. I am the widow of a nobleman who was too old for me to begin with. I did not expect you to take me for a virgin."

"Don't worry your pretty little head about it. I never did and, for the record, I ain't no virgin, neither."

She laughed weakly, gripping his shaft strongly, and said, "I needed a man. I expected you to be good in bed. I had no idea you would be *this* good. So now I am confused."

He told her he didn't want her to be confused. So he

got back aboard her to straighten her out. He figured she'd gotten over her moody Russian views on life and loving by the time they wound up. But as they were finishing she got to sobbing again about how she'd just never get enough of this by the time the ship docked.

He reached for his vest and fished out his pocket-watch. He sure hoped she was only joshing, for the boat didn't dock until three and it wasn't even lunchtime yet.

Chapter 2

She wept. She swore. She tore her hair. She promised to be true. She still threw him out an hour before the ship was due to dock so that she could get dressed and gussied properly. Neither what they'd been doing earlier nor the vodka he'd had for lunch on an empty stomach was doing much for Longarm's sea legs. He knew he would look even sillier walking like this on dry land. So he went to the side door of the galley and bet the dish-washing crew a dollar they couldn't find a trail herder's breakfast in the pantry.

He lost, of course, and he felt a lot more human after he'd cut open the cans and downed a pint of tomatoes and a pint of cold pork and beans. The salon served coffee all day long. After he'd put away plenty of strong black coffee he was just about ready to face the world again.

The *Sitka Sally* steamed up Sitka Sound, which looked

more like one of those Norway fjords Longarm had seen in a picture travel book, and he was smoking at the rail when they tied up to a dock running out into the silver-plated water. A U. S. Navy ironclad lay at anchor nearby with one of its turrets trained on Longarm, but he doubted it was meant personally. He saw naval personnel mixed in with the crowd on the dock. He looked over them at the so-called city of Sitka, clinging to the slopes like a Rocky Mountain mining camp. The hills behind the gray shingle roofing were covered with a thick green fuzz of second-growth spruce. The first settlers had clear-cut the original forest, but Nature didn't give up that easily where Pacific sea breezes watered the hillsides almost constantly.

He turned to take more interest in his closer surroundings as they lowered the gangway. Other passengers had of course stampeded into a bunch near the head of the gangway. As an experienced traveler, Longarm had learned long ago just to stay put and finish a smoke before he even thought about getting off whatever. He knew the boat wouldn't leave before everyone got off. From the way the others were pushing and shoving down yonder, they hadn't figured this out yet.

Debarking would have gone smoother had not some fussy gents in naval uniform been imitating Customs agents at the foot of the gangway. Longarm saw them fussing with Tasha about her considerable luggage. There was nothing he could do about it now, and it served her right for tossing a federal agent out of bed. But he stopped a passing deckhand to ask how come anyone had to go through Customs, getting off an American boat from an American port.

When the deckhand explained, Longarm felt sort of dumb. He'd paid little mind to the stops in British waters they'd made coming up the coast past British Columbia. Some Canadians had got off or on the steamer before it was back in American waters. What Canadians might be smuggling into Alaska eluded him, but those navy men on the dock figured to find whatever it might be. Longarm had had no idea Tasha carried that much vodka with her, no doubt for medicinal reasons. They hadn't even killed the one bottle they'd opened. So he couldn't help wondering just how long the Russian gal meant to stay in Sitka. The officer pawing through her luggage held at least a dozen bottles up to the light and checked the revenue seals carefully before he put everything back, closed Tasha's trunk lids for her, and saluted her. Tasha yelled something at some Indian boys standing back from the navy man and they came forward to pick up her gear. They were husky little runts, judging from how easily they could tote Saratoga trunks, and there was something about their bandy-legged walking style that reminded Longarm of Indians he knew better. He took a thoughtful drag on his cheroot, nodded, and muttered, "Yep, Nadene, sure as hell. But the so-called Apache are supposed to be on their reservations this summer, and they wasn't wearing paint. So I reckon she knows what she's doing."

It felt like a million years, but it was more like forty-five minutes later when Longarm decided it was time to drift aft and see if they'd let him off the boat. He hadn't brought anything along but a Gladstone packed with clean underwear and such. He had seen no need to bring along his Winchester or more than a couple of boxes of .44-40 ammonition for his sidearm and derringer. He picked up the bag and smoothed his frock coat open so the grips of his cross-draw Colt would show. It was better to let folk know you were packing hardware under your coat than to let them find out on their own and take it wrong. As he made sure the left-side pocket of his coat was likely to stay where it was he felt something in the pocket he didn't recall putting there. He looked down as he reached in, felt what seemed to be a string of beads, and hauled enough out into the light to gasp and shove them back hard. He had no idea where he could have picked up a string of uncut rubies, and he was being waved down the gangplank right now by a ship's officer.

He studied on what he ought to do about the mysterious jewelry in his pocket as he carried his innocent Gladstone down the gangway. Or was it innocent? He hadn't looked in the bag since the last time he'd changed into a fresh shirt, and Longarm didn't put on a fresh shirt every day. He decided he'd rather examine his own luggage than have some stranger do so. He got out his wallet and flashed his federal badge and I.D. at the lieutenant j.g. blocking the shoreward end of the gangway. The j.g. nodded and said, "We've been expecting you. Have you anything to declare?"

Longarm said, "Don't know. I ain't seen your prisoner yet."

"That's not what I meant. This territory is under U. S. Naval jurisdiction, and we're trying to run it right. You and the other passengers just arrived from a British port of call and so we must go through the usual formalities. So I repeat, have you anything to declare in the way of items that might require an import license of the payment of customs duties due the U. S. government?"

Longarm smiled, which always worked better in a poker bluff than a give-away poker face, and said, "I cannot tell a lie. I am a well-known international jewel thief trying to smuggle a quart or so of rubies in for sale to the stinking rich Tlinglits. I forget how many gold bars I got in this here Gladstone. There wasn't time to count as I robbed that bank in Seattle."

It worked. The j.g. looked disgusted and said, "Sure, they told us a wiseass from Justice was coming up the coast and to watch out for his sneaky sense of humor."

He turned to a husky c.p.o. and added, "Chief, take this cowboy clown to Commander MacLean. He might find him more amusing."

The c.p.o. grabbed Longarm's Gladstone and said, "Walk this way, sir."

Since the whole city of Sitka was in fact a village, it didn't take them long to get to the local navy brig, one of the only brick buildings in an otherwise highly inflammable town. The c.p.o. led Longarm into a bitty front office, dropped his bag on the cement floor, and told an older and even more spit-and-polish petty officer behind a judge-like bench that Longarm wasn't under arrest. The iron-gray desk wrangler said he knew all about it and picked up a Bell telephone speaker as the first one spun on one heel and marched out. After spinning the brass crank a few times, the man behind the desk got through to somebody and told him Longarm was ready to view the prisoner. Then he hung up, leaned back as comfortably as a man could sit without bending his spine an inch, and said, "The officers will be here in their own good time. Make yourself comfortable. You can smoke if you got 'em."

Longarm looked around, saw nothing to sit on, and said, "Look, I got a boat to catch back to the States. Why can't I just go back right now and see if you boys are holding Soapy Smith or some other gent?"

The c.p.o. looked shocked. "That's not the way things are done in the U. S. Navy. The suspect faces court-martial on a very serious charge."

"Hell, I know that. I'll bet even *he* knows that. But

we both know I won't be called as a witness if he ain't Soapy Smith, and there won't be no trial at all if he is."

The c.p.o. nodded sagely. "That's why they sent for you, Longarm. As soon as the defense and prosecution officers get here the matter will be settled one way or the other and you'll be free to go."

A steamship whistle moaned through the thick brick wall at them and Longarm demanded, "Go *where*, damn it? We're on an infernal *island* and they told me the *Sitka Sally* ain't fixing to stay here all that long."

"Don't you have a round-trip ticket?"

"Of course I bought a round-trip ticket. Did you think I come up here to marry an Eskimo and settle down for good? They told me they put in here once a week. I was hoping to go back aboard the same vessel. It only stays here long enough to unload and take on any cargo the forest elves may want to ship to the States. That whistle you just heard was telling us they've discharged their cargo and are ready to load up and get going. So I can still catch her home if you'll just take me back to the cellblock and let me eyeball that rascal for you, hear?"

The c.p.o. shook his head and replied, "I don't have the rank or the authority. If I did, you'd still have to wait and make a sworn statement to the proper officers."

"Well, pick up that infernal invention and call the officers' club some more, damn it. Let's get them proper officers off their proper dead asses so I can still catch my proper boat!"

The c.p.o. did no such thing. Longarm hadn't expected him to. He'd never served in the navy, but he knew old army noncoms could be a pain in the ass about pestering officers. You got to *be* an old noncom by kissing officers' asses, not pestering 'em.

Longarm lit a cheroot and commenced to pace the

floor like a caged tiger. If this bothered the old fool behind the desk he didn't let it show. He hauled out a paper-bound book and commenced to read it.

Longarm left his bag where it was and stepped outside to pace and smoke in the open air. He saw all sorts of stiff-backed navy men moving about in the middle distance. None of them seemed to be headed his way. He went around the side of the brig as if to take a leak. He made sure he was screened by the frame building next door and took out the mysterious string of rubies for another look-see. They were pigeon-blood uncut baroques, if they were real. They looked real, but Longarm was no jeweler and had no idea what they could be worth. That didn't bother him half as much as the fact that they'd wound up in his pocket uninvited. His first suspicion was obvious. He didn't remember Tasha slipping them in his duds while both of them were stark naked and actively engaged on the bed. But naturally no wicked woman bent on sneaking things into the pockets of her innocent prey would have announced her intentions as she did so. The frock coat had been hanging on the door hook in a mighty small stateroom. They hadn't spent all the time in bed, so it was possible.

But in that case, where had they come from? She hadn't even left her garters on as they made love, and he knew for sure she couldn't have had them concealed where so many she-male suspects tended to stuff compact contraband. Her long hair? Maybe. He'd run his fingers through it a lot, though. He put the rubies away again for now. The mystery of how she could have worked it was no more important than why she would have wanted to.

He moved around to the front of the brig. Still no officers in sight. He stomped his first smoked-down cheroot dead and lit another, muttering, "Let's see. She might have guessed her luggage would be searched, as it was. So she slipped me the crown jewels of Russia, figuring I wouldn't have to pass through Customs and that she could get 'em back the same way. Shit, that don't make sense."

He'd watched with his own eyes as the princess passed through Customs. They'd gone through the motions, but they hadn't really searched her personally. Had she hidden the rubies under her own duds, they'd have been as safe from seizure, and she wouldn't have had to go to the trouble of getting them back. Right?

Wrong. Any smuggler knew that if Customs agents really thought they had a reason to search a body, that body got searched. She could have been afraid to take the chance. There was no way in hell a smuggler was going to get caught with the goods on her if the goods were on someone else. She'd likely known before she picked him up that he was a federal agent who wasn't likely to be searched. He'd made no secret of his I.D., and the ship's purser was paid to answer questions.

"Sorry, Tasha." He sighed to his rising smoke as he saw how it worked better another way. The Russian gal never would have told him they couldn't get back together on shore if she'd had any intention of getting together with him to recover the jewels. Tasha hadn't been the only passenger on board. Anyone could have seen the same advantage and taken it. It would be even easier to drop something in the side pocket of a fully dressed gent with his brain a mite fuzzed and his balance aboard a moving ship not too steady. That worked better. It would look a lot easier to a smuggler just to pick a pocket later than it would to pick said pocket after telling its owner never to come near you again.

He saw a brace of navy brass headed his way along the cinder-paved path. He muttered, "It's about time, and Tasha ain't off the hook yet. She could have pulled that sad disavowal of future meetings to give herself an alibi. There's nothing in the U. S. Constitution saying a confederate can't pick a pocket for the one who put the goodies in it. So I wonder where Russian princess gals stay when they ain't seducing helpless dupes."

He had to put the jewelry on the back of the stove as the two officers greeted him warmly, considering how they'd made him wait. The three of them went inside. The c.p.o. led them back to the cellbloock. There was a screaming Indian locked in one cell. The only other prisoner that day was a white man with a full beard who clung to the bars and shouted, "It's about time you got here, Longarm! Tell these assholes who I am, and make 'em turn me loose, hear?"

He sure looked like Soapy Smith, and out on the water the *Sitka Sally* was calling to Longarm wistfully. But the tall deputy paid more attention to his duty than even his boss sometimes gave him credit for. So he nodded and said, "Afternoon, Soapy, maybe."

One of the naval officers sighed.

The prisoner jeered, "What did I tell you? I knowed my old pard, Longarm, would recall my handsome features. Unlock this durned door and let me loose, you sissy swabs!"

"Not yet," Longarm said. "The last time we met, if ever we did, you was smoother-shaved. Tell me about the last time we met, old son."

The prisoner frowned through the bars at him. "Oh, hell, if you want to rake up old grudges, I was only funning when I said I'd get you later. I'll admit I was a mite vexed with you at the time, but how was I to know

25

you'd ever be in a position to get me out of jail, Longarm, old pard?"

Longarm grinned crookedly. "Everything comes to he who waits, I reckon. I'm still waiting for you to tell me about the last time we met."

"Hell, don't *you* remember, Longarm? It was in that dinky saloon down by the Denver railyards. The discussion was over some rube you accused me of skinning."

"I never accused anyone. I said right out that a son of a bitch called Soapy Smith had rooked a poor country boy of his life savings."

The prisoner looked sheepish and said, "Yeah, but you made me give the money back. So tell these other sons of bitches to turn me loose."

"How about it, Longarm? Is he or isn't he?" one of the naval officers asked.

"Don't know yet. He looks like Soapy Smith and he talks like Soapy Smith. On the other hand, the affair got printed up in the *Denver Post* and I was sore as hell about it, too. My boss gave me pure ned for messing in a non-federal matter. I reckon we'd best ask this gent to take off his shirt."

"His *what?*" asked the other officer, who seemed to be on the defense team.

Longarm said, "Anyone could have read about the mild disagreement in the papers, and a man who looks like a well-known crook might have been teased in the past about the resemblance. I'd know better if this was the real Soapy Smith or just an admirer if he'd take off that shirt. So how come he's still got it on?"

The prosecution officer said, "You heard the man, Seaman Lee. Kindly remove that shirt."

"Hell, I told you I ain't no sailor named Lee, and it's cold in here, Lieutenant."

"It's not that cold, and I find it rather interesting that a Western badman who says he's never served in this man's navy is so familiar with the stripes on my sleeve. Get that shirt off. That's a direct order."

The prisoner swore under his breath, unbuttoned his shirt, and tossed it on the bunk beside him, muttering, "This is cruel and unusual punishment, but have your durn way. Let's get this over with, Longarm."

Longarm nodded. "It's over. You ain't Soapy Smith. You sure look like him, and I admire your balls. But a .44-40 slug leaves a considerable scar, even when I'm in a merciful mood, and you ain't wearing one. The real Soapy Smith has to be. For he slapped leather on me in Old Henry's Saloon and wound up in a corner nursing a sort of shot-up gun arm. It was a nice try, Seaman Lee. But as I told your hero, the real Soapy Smith, I'm smarter than any two crooks put together. Sorry about that."

The prisoner reached for his shirt, still protesting his innocence.

His defender swore and told him, "Now you're really in for it, you asshole! Didn't you expect a lawman who'd gunned the real Soapy Smith to remember it?"

The other officer, who had the easier job at the pending court-martial, chortled. "You're not just charged with desertion now, Lee. Didn't your mother ever tell you sailor boys get spanked for lying under oath to officers?" He turned to Longarm and added, "We'll need your sworn testimony at his court-martial now. As you see, he's slickered himself into a really long stretch of hard labor."

Longarm sighed. "Cuss me and my big mouth, too. I don't reckon there's any way of holding said trial before my boat leaves for Seattle."

The officer shook his head. "I'm afraid not. If you're talking about the *Sitka Sally*, it's already left port. But

27

don't worry. Commander MacLean means to have this idiot on the next steamer south, in leg irons. So you won't be stuck here more than, say, a week."

Chapter 3

Like all the other streets of Sitka, the main drag was cut out of a considerable slope. The frame buildings on either side were facing one another as if one row of saloons and such were standing on soap boxes and the others were standing in quicksand. The rutted street was narrow for a main drag and paved with coal cinders and wood ashes. They had to use something in such a wet climate, but the deeper ruts were still filled with water. Longarm tried to avoid puddles. He knew the lye leached from all that ash would play hell with his leather boots. Some of the locals sloshed right through in knee-high gumboots. Longarm figured they were either fishermen or loggers who'd had their original footgear eaten off their socks.

He had supper standing up at the steam table of a crowded saloon that served mighty salty stuff, free, in hopes of encouraging expensive thirsts. The price of drinks was outrageous up here. It was a small wonder Tasha

29

had brought her own vodka. The barkeep gave Longarm a dirty look when he ordered a single beer to wash down all the smoked salmon on rye he'd consumed. Longarm didn't see what he was fussing about. Beer cost a nickel less in Denver and came in a bigger glass as well.

He nursed his puny drink, belly to the bar, keeping an eye on the mirror behind it but giving anyone in the crowd every opportunity to pick his pockets. He'd put the rubies inside his shirt for safer keeping. He was trying to find out who might want them, not to give them up just yet. But nobody tried and, try as he might, Longarm had to finish the damned sissy beer sooner or later. As he turned away, the barkeep muttered, "Come back again, big spender. I told that fool Chinee to put more salt on the bread, but does anyone listen?"

Longarm resisted the impulse to suggest they might try chili con carne with plenty of salt, the way they did in Denver. He wasn't up here to teach folk how to run saloons.

He stepped out on the boardwalk and followed it until he found an assay office open. He went in and after he'd assured the worried-looking young gal behind the counter that he was law and not a holdup man, he reached inside his shirt and produced the string of rubies. He spread them on the glass and said, "I was wondering if you could tell me if these are real, ma'am."

The blonde hastily spread a square of fuzzy dark flannel on her counter and placed the necklace on it, saying, "Never put gem stones on glass, damn it."

"Does glass scratch rubies, ma'am?"

"No. It's the other way around. Just what sort of a deal did you have in mind, Deputy Long? My father would have to approve the sale if you mean to sell them, and he's not in town right now."

Longarm nodded. "That's all right. I don't aim to sell nothing. At the moment I'm holding these as possible evidence. I'd know better what they might be evidence of if I knew what they were worth. You say it's your father who's in charge of this assay office, not you?"

She looked hurt. "If I didn't know the trade I wouldn't have been left in charge. Frankly, I know more about precious metal that jewelry. But I guess I can tell real gem stones from paste!"

He nodded. "Go ahead, then, Miss, ah . . . ?"

"I'm Kathleen Snow and my friends *don't* call me Kate if they know what's good for them. You understand I can only give you a rough appraisal?"

"I sure wish you would, Miss Kathleen. Did your dad say when he'd be back, in case we need an expert?"

She reached under the counter for a jeweler's glass as she said, "My father's up in Juneau. It's a bitty mining camp you wouldn't have heard of. They've struck color, they think. Father's up there to tell them whether it's low-grade gold or pyrite. He'll be gone at least a few more days. But let's see what I can do for you."

She held the string up to the light and squinted at the pretty beads. She was sort of pretty, too, in a less flashy way. She examined stone after stone and must have been getting tired by the time she put them back on the jeweler's cloth. "They're worth something, as they're very high grade, but they're garnets, not rubies," she told him.

He frowned. "Are you sure? I thought garnets were more purple than red, Kathleen."

"I told you they were unusually *good* garnets. They sometimes come as red as rubies, making them more valuable as garnets and, as you see, a fair substitute for rubies. Unlike paste, garnet cuts glass like any other gem stone. So some dishonest jewelers have been known to

31

pass them off as low-quality rubies."

"I've noticed how dishonest some folk are. Are you saying that even if they was rubies, they wouldn't be so high class?"

"Heavens, they're riddled with flaws. That's why they haven't been cut, even as garnets. Tumble polished baroque can hide a multitude of sins. If these stones were worth cutting, even as garnets, they'd be worth a lot more. As they are, I'd say the string would fetch . . . oh, say five hundred dollars, if one could find a buyer more interested in flash than quality."

He frowned down at the pretty pebbles.

"I hope I haven't ruined your evening," she said. "How much did you pay for them?"

He smiled thinly and replied, "Nothing. And you say they're still worth almost as much as I make in a year. So this is getting curiouser and curiouser." He explained how he'd come by the mysterious stones, leaving out the dirty parts, and summed it all up by adding, "Five hundred dollars is a lot to an honest working man. It ain't enough for a really slick crook to tempt fate for and, in all modesty, I have a reputation for getting fatal to crooks. I've either been insulted professionsome or this was the work of a total fool. I don't know what in thunder I'm supposed to do with these almost-precious jewels now."

"Would you like us to keep them in our safe for you, Deputy Long?"

He started to say no. Then he wondered why he'd want to say a dumb thing like that. Nobody dealing regularly in gold and jewels figured to purloin one necklace, even if she was wrong about its value. The rascals who had to be planning on recovering them from him would have no way of knowing they'd been put away safe, and in case they did get the drop on him, it would be nice to know, at the end, that their plan hadn't worked. So he nodded and said he'd be much obliged and that he'd best leave her his home address in case he never got back alive to reclaim them.

As he tore out a sheet of notebook paper to write down Billy Vail's name and whereabouts she started to make out a receipt for him. He told her, "Don't bother. I know I can trust you better than I can trust anybody going through my pockets, and I don't want anyone but Marshal Vail ever to know who's got the mysterious gems."

She dimpled sweetly at him and wrapped the red garnets up to put them away. He asked her what he owed her. She said, "Don't be silly. It's an honor to assist the U.S. government. I had an uncle who fell in battle at Shiloh."

He nodded understandingly. He saw no call to tell such a pretty little thing he was old enough to be her uncle. Old war stories tended to be old bore stories to most women, in any case.

He waited until she'd dropped down on her haunches to put the uncut gem stones in the safe behind the counter. Her behind looked interesting, too, but he had another gal more on his mind at the moment. When she straightened up and turned around, brushing a wisp of hair from her brow, he said, "Now I got one more question. You have to know more about this town than me. So if you was looking for a newly arrived Russian, where would you start, Kathleen?"

She frowned thoughtfully. "There aren't many real Russians left in Sitka these days, if we're talking about white people. Some of the Tlingit converts still insist they're subjects of the Tsar. But you know how stubborn Indians can be."

"The ones I've seen so far look like a stubborn breed

33

indeed. But we're a mite far north for Apache, or as they call themselves, Nadene."

Kathleen blinked and said, "I never knew Apaches were Nadene. How could they be?"

"Just ask 'em polite, and they'll tell you if they're feeling polite. They can get sort of surly when you call 'em Apache. It's a Pueblo word meaning something like no darned good."

She laughed and said, "I've never met an Apache. But I know a lot of Tlingit, and *they* call themselves Nadene, too. Or at least that's what they call the language they speak. But how can that be? The Tlingit are salmon-fishing totem-pole Indians, Deputy Long!"

"I wish you'd call me Custis, Kathleen. As for Nadene further south, it stands to reason the so-called Apache had to come from somewhere, and all the southwest tribes agree they came busting down from the north about the time Columbus was arriving from the east. I reckon they had to give up fishing for salmon in the Arizona desert, and a totem pole carved out of cactus would just look silly. I'm glad you told me the local redskins are related to Indians I know all too well, though. It might make dealing with 'em up here easier."

"Be careful with Tlingit, Custis. Thanks to the Russians and a no-nonsense Indian policy, the Tlingit haven't been on the warpath for some time. But they still have a reputation for treachery."

"That's what I just said. I know how to get along with the breed as well as any white eyes can. You still ain't told me where to look for Russians."

She shrugged and said, "Well, the U. S. government's taken over the so-called Castle Baranov. There are some old-timers left up around thee so-called Cathedral of Saint

34

Michael. Look for a Russian cross on top of an overgrown log cabin. That'll be it."

He started to ask what a Russian cross looked like. Then he remembered. An Orthodox church in Denver had that gilt cross with an extra little crossbar. He asked her how late she stayed open.

She said until nine and asked why.

"I might want to get the jewels out of your safe if I can find someone to own up to 'em," he said. "But they can wait till morning. Don't stay open late for me."

She said she'd stay open until midnight and when he told her not to be silly she insisted she had nothing better to do. So he left. He'd learned long ago that life was too short to spend much of it arguing with stubborn women.

He strode along the boards until he spied a husky Indian who didn't seem to be in a hurry, and stopped him to ask directions to the old Russian mission. The Tlingit smelled like he'd had more to drink that night than one could tell, just watching him walk. He scoweled at Longarm and demanded, "Who wants to know, White Eyes? You don't look like a follower of the True Faith. You look like a woman-heart who sits down to pee!"

Longarm smiled pleasantly and replied, "My heart soars to meet a Nadene looking for a good fight. But before I spit in your eye and drown you, little brother, does your mother know you are out so late?"

The big Indian looked more startled than enraged as he sobbed, "You have mentioned my mother, and for that you must die. But before I rip your arms and legs off as one deals with butterflies, who told you I was a real person?"

"Isn't that what Nadene means? If I've mistaken an

Eskimo for a Tlingit we'd best say no more about it. I hardly ever stomp Eskimo. I only fight Nadene. For they are my favorite enemies."

"Hey, you know how good we fight, eh?"

"Sure I do. If I didn't fight *better* we wouldn't be having this tedious discussion. So, do you want to get your ass whipped, or do you want to tell me where Saint Michael's is?"

"I have to think about this. What if I showed you the way and waited for you outside? That way you could make your last confession to the priest and die pure under the spruce limbs. It is very dark out that way. Nobody would come along to spoil our fight, see?"

Longarm said that sounded reasonable. The Tlingit led him off the main drag and up a side street so dark Longarm wasn't sure his guide meant to wait for the fight he was spoiling for. By the time they were within sight of the lights of the old Russian mission the Tlingit was having a little trouble staying on his feet. Longarm grabbed his arm as he started to fall through a picket fence and said, "Steady, chief. Why don't we just find a place to set you down, sedate?"

"I am not a chief. I am a boat steerer. I am called Killer Whale With Raven On His Shoulder. You can just call me Killer Whale, like everyone else does. Where do you want me to wait for you?"

Longarm looked around, found a spruce stump nobody was using for anything better, and sat Killer Whale on it. "I got to come back this way. So it's up to you whether I find you waiting here or not. If I was you I'd sleep on the notion. You're too drunk to fight."

"Bullshit! Killer Whale is always spoiling for a fight. Ask anyone."

Longarm let go and the Indian went over backwards

to sprawl helpless on the soggy grass. The big lawman grimaced and went on up to the cathedral.

It was fancier inside. That wasn't hard to manage. Longarm removed his Stetson and moved respectfully along a side aisle toward the candle-lit gold-plated altar. He didn't make it. A bearded gent dressed in a sort of chef's uniform, only black, popped out between some drapes to demand his name and business. Longarm flashed his I.D. and a friendly smile. So Brother Boris, as the gent in the funny hat turned out to be, conducted him next door to where an older and even funnier-dressed gent said he was the bishop in charge of the whole show. He sat Longarm down on a sofa, poured him a glass of red wine, and sat across from him to ask what the U. S. government might want of the Eastern Orthodox Church.

Longarm told him, "Nothing direct, since it's a free country, sir. I'm looking for one of your people in connection with some mysterious jewelry."

"Oh, dear, I hope none of our poor Indians have been accused of jewel theft, Deputy Long."

"Not hardly, sir. But while we're on the subject, are you telling me all your parish here is Tlingit?"

"We have a few whites left from the old days, Deputy Long. But most went home when our Little Father, for some strange reason, saw fit to sell this land to you."

"Your Tsar didn't sell Alaska to me direct, Bishop. By the way, has the B.I.A. seen fit to establish an agency up here yet?"

"B.I.A., my son?"

"Bureau of Indian Affairs. Let's not worry about that. I can see they ain't if *you're* still riding herd on the local Indians. I ain't worried all that much about Indians, neither. I'm looking for a paler Russian gal who calls herself the Princess Natasha Baranov."

"She must be an impostor," said the old man, flatly.

Longarm asked, "Do you know her, sir?"

The bishop shook his head and beard. "I don't have to. No such person exists. I have been here longer than you could have been alive, my son, and I remember the last Russian governor and his family well as well as fondly. They had no daughter named Natasha."

"Do tell? What about the princess part?"

The old Russian smiled thinly. "A princess or a prince is not hard to find in Russia. Anyone who owns more than a dozen horses tends to call himself a prince."

Longarm frowned and asked, "Is that lawful, sir? Seems to me a prince ranks just under a king, most places. So they couldn't be all that common, even allowing for a big royal family."

The old Russian sighed and said, "That is the trouble with trying to translate our language into English or even French. You see, the word you know as prince derives from the Latin, meaning 'the first.' Do you not, in English, refer to things as first class?"

Longarm nodded and then brightened to say, "Oh, I follow your drift. In Russia any big shot is called first class so that comes out . . . Hold on, what do you call a *real* Russian prince?"

"Tsarovitch. Son of the Tsar."

"Then in Russia calling yourself a prince don't mean near as much as it might say in England?"

The bishop shrugged. "In my country 'prince' is simply a title of respect. You might translate it as country squire, but of course in dealing with you people, our merely rich must find it more impressive to use the word prince. This woman calls herself a princess, and dares to assume the good name of Baranov?"

"Well, don't get your bowels in an uproar, Bishop. I

figured she might be fibbing. As soon as I catch up with her I'll tell her you don't back her play worth much. It's been good talking to you and I thank you for your interesting lesson in Russian customs. Now I'd best get cracking and teach that sassy gal some manners, U. S.-style."

Brother Boris showed Longarm out, either to keep him from getting lost or to prevent him from swiping a candle. As he headed back to the main drag Longarm hoped he wouldn't run into an Indian spoiling for a fight.

He didn't. There were at least half a dozen Tlingit standing in a silent sullen knot around the stump where he'd left Killer Whale. Killer Whale was still sprawled on the wet grass, cussing or snoring—it was hard to tell. Longarm wasn't looking for any sort of fight with any sort of half dozen full-grown men. But if the Indians up this way took things so seriously, it was better to get it over with. He just kept walking and, sure enough, one of them stepped out into his path, so he stopped to see what happened next.

The Indian facing him was shorter than Killer Whale but built like a pit bull. He growled like a fighting dog, too, as he asked, "Are you really the one they call Longarm?"

"I fear I must be, since I ain't met anyone else called that in recent memory. Is my Nadene brother asking friendly, or am I glad as hell I brought my gun along this evening?"

Some of the other Tlingit sucked in their breaths, hissing like sidewinders on the prod. But the one blocking his path seemed calm enough as he replied, "If you are Longarm, why is Killer Whale still alive? When we heard he had walked out into the trees with a white eyes, and who the white eyes was, we came here to see who needed to be buried first. He is still alive. He is so drunk he should be ashamed of himself, but he has not been injured in any other way. How could this be so, Longarm?"

The white man shrugged. "I only fight when I have to. You can all see that poor drunken brute ain't in shape to fight a little girl."

"That is true. But Killer Whale is a man of reputation. Would it not add to your reputation as an Indian fighter if you killed such a wild Indian?"

Longarm chuckled. "Hell, I've lost count on how many Indians I've had to kill. Some of them was Nadene, by the way. But I killed 'em fair, in good fights. I've yet to kill any man, red or white, who didn't need killing. So tell me who you might be and whether you need killing or just a pistol-whipping, if you don't get the hell out of my way!"

The pack leader laughed in a surprisingly boyish way and said, "You have spoken to Nadene before, I can see. I am sorry you were not here the last time we took the warpath. It would have been a good fight. I am called Wolverines Fear His Smell. You can call me Big Stink, as other white eyes do. I am not at war with your kind this summer. You did not take advantage of my drunken brother, even though you have a gun and they would not hang you for using it on one of us. I think I will let you live, Longarm."

"You think you got much choice, Big Stink?"

"Don't push it. We are both men of reputation. Neither of us can back down too much. Neither of us wants trouble right now. I think we had better leave it at that."

Longarm nodded soberly. "So be it. War's over with honors to both sides and I'll even walk part way around you if you'll stand part way aside."

Big Stink did so. But as Longarm passed he murmured, "Watch out for Killer Whale when he sobers up. The others are sure to laugh at him about this affair, and *he* is a man of reputation, too!"

"I savvy your meaning. Will you have to avenge him if need be?"

"Of course. That is why it would be unwise of you to kill him."

Chapter 4

Sitka was way the hell west as well as way the hell north of Denver. So, knowing the home office would have closed for the day before he had arrived, Longarm had seen no reason to wire Billy Vail up to now. But there was always the chance Billy had wired him, and he had some bitching of his own to do now. If he sent his protests about the U. S. Navy by the cheaper night letter rates he'd not only save the taxpayers money, but Billy would find it waiting for him when he got up to wake the roosters of Denver.

Finding the Western Union office in such a small town was no big deal. The clerk on duty said there were no messages waiting for him. Longarm frowned thoughtfully and said, "That's odd. My boss is an old mother hen and he gets to wire on other folks' money. Are you sure your wire to the States is up?"

"I just took a message from New York City. Ain't no

way to send dots and dashes through the *air,* you know."

"I've been meaning to ask you just how your wires are strung, in case I have to follow 'em south. Ain't we out on an island?"

The clerk nodded. "We are. We reach the mainland by underwater cables. Then the wires go over the coast ranges to the Canadian system. Western Union serves all sorts of funny places."

"You mean your telegraph lines don't go down the coast? How do you wire Seattle from here?"

"The long way around, of course. Electricity travels lickety-split and you don't string any more copper wire through Tlingit country than you have to. Them Indians set great store by copper. They think it's worth more than gold. The Canadian Mounties have more control on the inland tribes. Nobody has any control on the confounded Tlingit. Our wire crews have tales to tell, just getting through *some* of 'em. Western Union finally managed to make a deal with old Katchatag or we wouldn't be able to stay in business at all."

"I'll bite. Who's Katchatag?"

"Chief of the Tlingit betwixt here and the less pain-some Indians to the east. Like I said, the Tlingit are crazy for copper. But the company managed to convince old Katchatag it made more sense for him to accept a yearly tribute in copper ingots than to gather his own off our poles."

Longarm frowned and said, "I ain't sure the B.I.A. would approve of such blackmail. But it ain't my business, unless they ask for me to step in. What's to stop lesser Tlingits from collecting copper wire on their own, pard?"

The clerk smiled incredulously and said, "Katchatag. He ain't no plain old Indian chief. He's a *big* chief. So

44

even us whites have to do as he says on his own ground and no Tlingit born of mortal squaw is about to disobey him. But don't worry about your night letter. I don't think the old man likes us much, but he's a man of his word, and we just sent him some more copper."

Longarm wasn't ready to write on the message form yet. "I can see your position gives you an ear to the local ground and I'm glad you ain't one of them secretive Western Union gents I have to pistol-whip secrets out of. While we're on the subject of precious metals, I just heard a tale of gold in them thar hills. Or at least I hear they think they've spotted color in a place called Juneau. Tell me about it."

The clerk looked disgusted. "I send a dozen wires a week about gold in Alaska. If any old sourdough tries to sell you a map in a saloon, save your money for booze. There's more booze than gold in Seward's Folly. But it's sort of expensive."

"I noticed. I've still heard of gents panning gold in them coast ranges to the east. Stands to reason there has to be some color in 'em, since they're an extension of the California ranges that ain't given out on gold as yet."

The clerk shook his head and said, "Flashes in the pan, is all. It ain't like nobody's tried, you know. You ain't the first pilgrim to notice the whole Pacific coast is sort of bumpy. There's copper all over the place. The Indians were mining it afore we got here. There's a little low-grade gold ore hither and yon. No placer rich enough for small operators. We keep hearing tall tales about placer gold in the interior. An old boy staggered in a few years back with a gold poke in his fist and a Tlingit arrow in his back. Said he'd spent a summer panning some creek calt the Yukon. If so, it didn't do him much good. Besides, the only Yukon on the somewhat uncertain maps is in Canadian territory. So what the hell."

Longarm shrugged, said he hadn't been sent to investigate mining claims in any case, and wrote out a curt message to Marshal Vail, asking him to get the infernal U. S. Navy sunk or at least off his back. He handed it across the counter. "Two more questions?"

"Shoot. I got nothing better to do this late at night."

"You said the big chief of the Tlingit is a gent I can't pronounce. Have you ever heard tell of a chief called Big Stink?"

The clerk nodded. "Watch out for him. He's a bad Injun. He tells the breeds and mission Indians around here what to do and it's usually something sneaky. But the real Tlingit Nation ain't too impressed with a gent who talks English and goes to pray in Russian. According to the unreconstructed Tlingit, God is a big bird. Old Katchatag don't hold with drinking as much as Big Stink and his fishermen do, neither. It's funny how every religion always seems to forbid one damn pleasure or another. To give the devil his due, Big Stink and his gang kick the liver and lights out of any white man fooling with a Tlingit squaw. Then they go have a drink on it. Old Katchatag has been knowed to shoot a bottle out of a man's hand and swears booze is poison. Yet the gals in native dress are said to screw like mink and nobody seems to care. That's how you can tell if it's safe to mess with an Indian squaw in these parts. If she's dressed half white, leave her the hell alone. If she's draped in a cedar-bark chilkat and don't run away, it's likely safe to offer her some copper pennies and screw her. Ain't Indians confusing?"

Longarm grimaced and said, "We likely confuse *them,* some. Next question. I'm looking for a white gal who calls herself the Princess Baranov. Has she sent or picked

46

up any wires from the States as yet?"

The clerk reached for a ledger, gave up the notion as pointless, and said, "Nope. I'd remember a princess. What did she look like? I've had six or eight gals send wires home this evening. Mostly fancy-looking soiled doves who wire money home regular. If you want to know how to dig gold in Alaska, ask a woman. They seem to arrive with a natural gold mine betwixt their legs, the sassy things."

Longarm described Tasha.

The clerk shrugged. "Brunettes ain't that unusual, even in a town where womankind is a rare species. I'd have remembered one with a furren accent. It's hard enough to get the messages right when they talk plain English. What kind of a message would she be sending or receiving?"

"If I knew that, I wouldn't be so puzzled about her. She can't be who she says she is, and anyone can sound French if they put their mind to it. All I know for sure is that someone's trying to pull a flimflam on me, and so far I ain't got nobody else to discuss it with. I thank you for your time and friendly words. But I ain't about to find that princess here. So I'd best be going."

He tried the hotels next, or at least he tried what passed for hotels in Sitka. They looked more like rooming houses to him. That made it easier to establish Tasha didn't seem to be staying at any of them. It was harder to check in sneaky when the place had a landlady blocking the cabin door instead of a desk clerk in a lobby one could maneuver in. He made mental notes on the cleaner-looking ones with less ferocious landladies as he canvassed the local inns. He still had no idea where he was supposed to bed down, once it got late enough. His possibles had been left in care of the navy past the brig. But he didn't

47

think he wanted to sleep there and they hadn't offered him a room.

When he ran out of rooming houses and ideas he checked the time and saw it was pushing ten. He remembered the gal at the assay office had said she'd wait up for him. In case she had, it was time he told her not to. He wasn't about to find Tasha before he caught up on his own sleep.

He strode down to the assay office and sure enough found it open. He stepped inside and Kathleen Snow looked up hopefully from some rocks she was grinding in a mortar. He smiled sheepishly down at her and said, "I just bottomed out. The whereabouts of the mysterious Russian gal is still a mystery."

He brought her up to date on his adventures and added, "I don't know about you but I have to study on a place to turn in for the night. I hardly ever sleep in the rain and it's getting sort of soggy outside now."

She nodded and said, "The mists blowing in from the sea will have everything dripping by morning. I wish I knew of a decent hotel in Sitka, but I don't think there is one."

She poured some of the pulverized ore into a test tube, poured something from a bitty brown bottle in with it, and held the whole mess up to the light so she didn't have to meet his eyes as she added, sort of breathlessly, "I suppose we could put you up *here* for the night. We've a guest room upstairs, Custis."

She had a father out of town on business, too. Longarm knew his own nature and suspected her of being blonde all over. But he was a lawman first. He knew his badge didn't cover shooting outraged fathers and he was damned if he could figure out any other way to handle a man coming home to find his only daughter in bed with a total stranger. So he sighed as if he took her offer seriously and said, "I'd best check in to the B.O.Q. at the naval base. Got to get up at the crack of dawn, and—"

"I'm an early riser, Custis," she cut in.

He was starting to rise a mite early himself. So he told a fib about having to jaw with at least an admiral before bedtime and got the hell out of there while they were still pure. From the way she threw her test tube on the floor and stomped it as he was going out the door he sort of doubted purity was what she'd had in mind. She was pretty, too, cuss her reckless hide.

Having lied about the B.O.Q., Longarm decided he might as well check it out. He walked around the harbor to the naval base and got as far as a sailor boy guarding the gate with a pea jacket, a rifle, and his life, to hear him tell it. He said nobody was allowed on the base without an invitation after dark.

Longarm got tired of waving his badge and I.D. at the fool. He put his wallet away and said, "Let me explain from the beginning, sonny. I was just in that brig we both can see from here, this very evening. You know and I know there's a petty officer hatching eggs just inside that lit-up front window. So why don't we ask him if it's all right for me to come aboard?"

"Sorry, sir. I can't leave my post."

"Well, what if I was to just step around you and go knock on that door for you?"

The younger man looked serious as he said, "You'd never make it. I have orders to shoot anyone who tries to get by me, sir."

He sounded like he meant it and Longarm didn't think Justice would approve his slapping leather on the Navy Department. So he suggested, "Why don't we try it this way? You call the corporal of the guard or whatever the hell you naval guards call him and let *him* decide whether I can come in out of the cold or not. It's getting misty as hell now, old son."

The guard nodded. "That's why they issued me this pea jacket, sir. You'd best go back to town before it *really* starts misting."

"Have you got wax as well as mist in your ears, boy? Call your infernal superior and let's get this dumb conversation over with."

The guard shook his sailor hat. "My first general order is to walk my post in a military manner and so forth. I'm to call for assistance only should an unusual case I can't handle on my own arise and, no offense, I think I can handle you, sir."

Longarm scowled. "You know what you are? You're a pissant, that's what you are. We had sentries like you in the old army and we called *them* pissants, too! What in thunder are you bucking for, seaman second?"

"I'm only doing my duty, sir."

"I noticed. I'm good at remembering faces, even in this light, and if I die of pneumonia I mean to come back and haunt you good!"

He turned away and headed back to the lights of Sitka, repressing a shiver fit. His longjohns were packed away in his Gladstone. His Gladstone was in the brig, where he couldn't get at it without declaring war on the U. S. Navy. He decided he needed a roof over his head, pronto. So the first place he stopped was the first saloon he came to.

It was a lot warmer inside, in more ways than one. Proper gals were not served in saloons, so the gals against the bar or holding the upright piano upright with the bare elbows couldn't be mistaken for thirsty schoolmarms.

50

Longarm pushed through the men dressed rougher, as well as more, and bellied up to the bar to order Maryland rye or, if that didn't work, anything strong enough to save a wayfaring stranger from pneumonia on such a cold unfriendly night. The female barkeep served him unbranded redeye and said she could get friendly as hell if he wanted to wait till she got off around three in the morning. He smiled down at the view and gently informed her he wasn't allowed to stay up that late, much as he might want to. She didn't get mad. He hadn't expected her to. Barmaids seldom put out. They had no call to, since they could get good tips just by acting like they might.

As he was inhaling his second drink a gal on his side of the mahogany moved her silk-sheathed hip against his and husked, *"I* like to go to bed early, too, big boy. They call me Frenchy. Do you like French lessons, big boy?"

He chuckled fondly down at her, despite how awful she looked, and said, "Ain't life a bitch? You'd just never believe how often I've been stuck in a strange town, looking for female companionship, without a female to be found. So naturally, now that I has my own true love awaiting me just down the street, I have to run into a pretty little thing like you."

"And *me,*" added the better-looking barkeep with a wink, now that she knew it was safe. Frenchy said, "I got the advantage on you, Doris. So just keep out of this. I'm sure our mutual friend is man enough for a quickie. Ain't that right, big boy?"

Longarm shook his head. "Alas, I know my own too-mortal flesh too well, Miss Frenchy. You're just too pretty for a man of my weak nature to make casual love to. We both know my true love would be forgotten until she wound up mad as hell by the time I got home. So I thank you kindly, but I gave my word I'd return to my true love early. It's been nice talking to you, but..."

But then the desperate whore had her arms around him and was trying to pin him against the bar with her thrusting pelvis as she pleaded, "Come on, big boy, three ways for two dollars and we can make it quick, if you're man enough!"

The barkeep warned her, "Cut that out, Frenchy. The man said no, and I try to run this place decent." Then her blue eyes widened as she saw even more disgusting action about to take place. She shouted, "Cowboy, duck!" as a bearded man in a floppy felt hat went for the Patterson Conversion under his sheepskin coat, staring wild-eyed at Longarm as he drew.

Longarm went for his own gun. It wasn't easy with the gal plastered against him, but he got his .44 out just in time to return the other man's first and only shot. Longarm's round took the stranger over the heart and sent him reeling back to crash down on a table and scatter poker chips and poker players in every direction. As the bulky corpse rolled off the table to thud to the sawdust, the saloon cleared of innocent bystanders faster than it cleared of gunsmoke. The whore who'd been pushing against him seemed to be confused as hell about the situation. For she was sliding down Longarm to her knees. Then she fell over backwards to lie sprawled at his feet like a broken doll. Longarm kept his gun trained on the man he'd just put on the floor farther off as he dropped to one knee to feel Frenchy's throat. Her heart was still pulsing weakly. Doris came around the end of the bar and dropped to her own knees in the sawdust to hold Frenchy's head in her lap. She told Longarm, "She caught a round I suspect was meant for you. How come?"

Longarm muttered, "Don't know. I'm law and it's

hard to tell who a man might be, with a beard I disre-
member tangling with in the past."

The whore on the floor between them fluttered her
eyes open and he asked her, "Where are you hit, Frenchy?
I don't see nothing on this side of you."

She murmured, "Somebody shoved a hot poker through
my ribs from ahint, and the light's sure dim in here right
now."

He placed the .44 on the sawdust nearby and gently
put his hand under her satin-clad torso. He felt the blood
pulsing out in steady spurts. He looked up at Doris. "We
need a doc, fast."

The barkeep murmured, "We sent for one, and I think
you're wrong."

Longarm wasn't about to argue with her about that.
The sawdust seemed to be soaking up the blood as fast
as she could bleed, but old Frenchy was pale as a sheet
now, and how much blood could a bitty whore have inside
her to begin with? As they held her bleakly, not knowing
what else to do, Frenchy looked up at Longarm and said,
"No shit, handsome. Did you really mean what you said
about me being a mighty tempting opportunity?"

He nodded gravely and replied, "I never lie to a lady,
Miss Frenchy. Had not that rascal discontinued our conversation so rude, I reckon I never would have made it
home tonight."

"You're not just shitting me? I know I ain't as pretty
as I was when I commenced this line of work, but I do
give mighty good service, and I told you you could have
it cheap."

"You don't look cheap, Miss Frenchy. I'm sure you
was just funning when you said two dollars. You know
you meant to get at least twenty out of me once you had
me in your wicked power and, to tell the truth, I'd have

had to give it to you. I told you I was weak-natured when it come to pretty gals."

She closed her eyes, but her whore's brain was still working to the last. "Easy to say. I don't see no twenty dollars, big spender."

Longarm reached in his pants with his other hand and dug out a gold double eagle, saying, "Here it is, honey. So now you'd best get well so's we can do all sorts of sassy things together, hear?"

He placed the coin in her limp left palm. She gripped it tightly, weakly raised it to her mouth, and bit it. Then she said, "Son of a bitch! My tail's still worth a double eagle! Ain't that a bitch?"

Then she shuddered, gasped, and went limp as a wet rag. Doris gave an odd little giggle and said, "Jesus, she swallowed the gold and now she's dead! How will you ever get it back now, lawman?"

Longarm smiled ruefully and said, "Ain't no way. My friends call me Custis, by the way."

"You must have a lot of friends if you're in the habit of dropping gold around. That's over two weeks' day wages you just wasted. Don't that bother you?"

He shrugged. "I'm still alive to make more money. She ain't. Maybe it's fitting she'll be buried with the wages of another's sins. I suspicion she'd have enjoyed the notion."

"I suspicion you're a gallant fool! You think I couldn't tell you were just being polite to an ugly old whore, Custis?"

"Maybe so, but she was dying. What was I supposed to act like, *rude?*"

Before Doris could answer boot heels clumped in to join them. A gent with a copper badge announced himself as the town law and told Longarm to get up slow with his hands preceding him. Doris snapped, "Don't be an asshole, you asshole. This one's law, too, and he outranks you. The one you want to arrest is that critter in the sheepskin yonder."

The townee moved over, rolled the corpse on its back with his toe, and observed, "Can't arrest *this* one, Miss Doris. He's dead as a smoked salmon caught last winter. I wish someone would tell me what this was all about."

Another man came forward to bend over Frenchy. He opined, "This one's dead, too." Doris introduced him as a local doctor. Longarm didn't argue with his medical opinion. He let go of the dead whore, picked up his .44, and proceeded to reload as he got to his feet and moved over to join the town law near the other stiff. The copper badge had meanwhile bent to remove a wallet from inside the sheepskin coat. He opened it and read off, "Hiram H. Hammond, registered to vote in Kansas City, according to his card. Can't say as I've ever heard of the rascal."

Longarm stared down at the slack-jawed, bearded face and said, "That ain't his real name. But the fliers on him said he might be using a voter's card missing from a victim called Hammond. Given that hint, I recognize him, now, as the late Wabash McRoy, wanted for armed robbery and other crimes too numerous to mention. He must have thought it was safer up Alaska way. When he recognized me first in an Alaska saloon, he might have thought I was after him. I have a reputation for being sent unusual distances after unusually wanted outlaws. By the way, I'd best show you my own badge and I.D."

The town law glanced idly at Longarm's open wallet, then blinked and gasped, "My God, you're the one they calls Longarm! It's no wonder this old boy tried to gun you! There's no *might* about it. He *had* to think you was after him!"

Longarm put the I.D. away. "Maybe old Wabash was a hired gun in life. So I'd best keep an open mind about his motives. I know for a fact the Pinkertons have posted five hundred dollars on him. That ain't no good to me. I ain't allowed to claim bounties and when I shoots a man in the field I'm supposed to bury him at my own expense unless some other lawman would like him as a present."

The older town law raised a thoughtful eyebrow and said, "Say no more, Longarm. I distinctfully recall deputizing you to round this rascal up for me, earlier this evening. You couldn't have been acting in your federal capacity, since the only federal law up here is the durned old navy, right?"

"I was hoping you'd see things that way. Most do. It cost me forty whole dollars of my own money to get rid of a dead breed in Montana nobody else on earth had any use for. Why don't you wire the Pinks about their dead-or-alive offer and say as little as possible about how he wound up dead. I'm sure the Pinks won't care. They was mad as hell at him."

They shook on it and Longarm turned around to see how Doris and Frenchy were making out. Some other townees were carrying the dead gal out. The still living barkeep was leaning against her bar, looking upset. Longarm went over to join her. "Cheer up. Things'll get back to normal here as soon as word gets about that the shooting is over for the night."

Doris grimaced. "I'm closing, as soon as they drag that other one out and give me a chance to spread more sawdust. I just ain't up to no more smiling and winking tonight, Custis. Frenchy was a pest and I didn't know that other cadaver at all, but this whole mess has left me depressed as hell. I'm about to have me a drink. You want to join me?"

He said sure and reached in his pocket. Doris told him not to be a fool and jumped up to swing her legs across the bar. He noticed she had nice legs. He'd already seen more of her tits than the law allowed in more proper townships. The rest of her was sort of standard, save for too much makeup. Her big blue eyes didn't need all that shoe-blackening around them and her hair, while no particular shade of brown, was thick and clean-looking.

She placed two beer schooners on the mahogany between them. Longarm admired beer well enough. He was a mite taken aback when she produced a bottle of expensive bourbon and preceeded to fill both big schooners. He gulped and said, "I'll do my best. But don't hold me to any promises to make it out the door on my own, after."

She shrugged. "Drink what you like and leave what you don't. You've no idea how tired I get of pouring a shotglass at a time."

They clinked on it and took a stiff mutual belt. He put his own down with a strangled gasp and managed, "Good stuff. But I'd best take it slow. What happened to all them other gals I saw in here earlier, Miss Doris?"

She said, "I run a saloon, not a whorehouse. Frenchy and them others takes gents home to raise. The custom was established before we bought the place. The original owners rented cribs by the minute upstairs. I don't. I run it as decent as you can run a place like this in a town like this."

He took a more gingerly sip of bourbon. "You're mixing me up with the plural and singular, Miss Doris.

When you say 'we,' who are we talking about?"

She sighed softly. "I come up here from Oregon with a husband. Now I'm running the place alone."

"Oh, sorry. What happened to him, if it ain't too painful to talk about?"

"Beats the shit out of me. Some say he ran off with an Indian gal. Some say he went off to pan for gold and the Indians got him. It ain't as painful for me as it'll be for him if he ever dares to show his face around here again. I don't mind telling you it hasn't been easy, paying off his debts and keeping this business afloat. Now that the books are in the black again, it'll be a cold day in hell before I let any sweet-talking man share my profits with me again."

He looked away. He saw they were alone, now. The saloon looked a lot larger, empty. The blackness beyond the batwing doors looked sort of spooky too. "Well, I'd best be on my sweet-talking way so you can close up," he said.

She put down the schooner she'd been drinking from and said, "I need help with the shutters. I generally get a strong-looking customer to help me with 'em. You'll have to do, tonight. So don't go yet."

He shrugged. "Can we have less light on the subject, then? I can't say for sure that gent who tried to kill me earlier come to Alaska alone, and I sure would be an easy target from outside right now."

Doris nodded, turned around, and let the central ceiling fixture down by its ingenious block and tackle gear from behind the bar. Longarm stepped out to trim the six oil lamps. It was a lot darker as she hauled them back up by the light of the single lamp over the bar. She reached up to trim it low and in the resulting ruby glow she giggled and asked, "What would your true love say if she came down the street to find you drinking in the dark with a shady gal like me?"

He chuckled and said, "I don't have a true love waiting for me anywhere tonight. Packing a badge and having true loves don't go together too well."

Doris frowned at him in the gloom. "How come you told Frenchy . . . ?" Then she brightened. "You *are* a sweet-talking man. The poor old thing had got long past the stage where even drunks was polite to her. How come you treated her so decent?"

He shrugged. "Before she got to be an old bawd she was likely a little girl. As you just saw, I sometimes have to kill folk in my line of work. It don't hurt to be decent when you can to fellow human beings, Miss Doris."

She wiped her eyes. "I can see you'd never make a living as a saloon owner. Where are you staying tonight, if you were fibbing about your true love?"

"I ain't decided yet. Like you said, I was just being decent to Miss Frenchy."

"Oh? What if she'd been better looking, and more interested in pure friendship than money?"

"Don't know. I ain't had such an offer yet."

Doris laughed, took a healthy belt of bourbon, and said, "Like hell you ain't. Help me shutter yonder front door and I'll show you where you'll be sleeping tonight, and with whom."

Chapter 5

Longarm didn't get all that much sleep once he was in bed upstairs with Doris. She started out demure enough. She just took him to her quarters and undressed by candle-light as if they were old pals getting together again after a spell apart. He liked gals who took such a natural approach to acting natural. She didn't even raise a fuss when she helped him out of his own duds and saw what he had to offer. She just gazed fondly down at his raging erection and murmured, "Oh, nice. I was hoping you'd be tall all over."

Then she shoved him over backwards, cocked a bare leg over, and impaled herself on his shaft with a contented sigh. When he rolled atop her to finish right she smiled up at him and said, "Oh, yes, that's the way it feels best."

When they stopped for a smoke and some friendly pillow talk, she asked him calmly how long he meant to be in town. He waited until he'd lit up and she was taking a drag on the cheroot before he said cautiously, "Don't know. The infernal navy wants me to testify about matters I know next to nothing about at a court-martial I ain't interested in. They tell me the next steamer south don't leave for a week. If it's at all possible to leave here sooner, I mean to—no offense."

"None taken," she replied, snuggling closer. "I know *I* wouldn't want to spend a week I didn't have to in this nowheres-much. You want to stay here with me as long as you're in town?"

He had to answer that cautiously indeed. "I'd admire that, and you know it. But we'd best work out some ground rules, honey."

She shrugged her bare shoulder and said, "I see no need for rules and regulations, lover. You know where I work and when I close shop. I'll give you a spare key. You just come in the back way any time you like and if I'm not up here when you want to turn in, hell, you can start without me."

"Just like that? I know this is no time to dwell on past romances, Doris, but some gals seem to feel used and abused when a gent treats 'em like . . . ah . . ."

"Port in the storm?" she asked. "That's what I am, ain't I? Have I asked you for any promises or, God forbid, *money?*"

"No, but do you feel this is fair to you, Doris?"

"You screw fair indeed, and what gives you the notion the pleasures are confined to one sex, Custis? Sure, I know you're just using me. Maybe I'm just using you, too. I enjoy getting laid. But I'd be a fool to mess with my regular customers or even a navy man, stationed here permanent. We've each got what the other wants—a discreet, friendly screw whenever neither of us is busy doing something more important. What else do you want?"

He laughed, snuffed out the smoke, and took her in his arms again as he said, "Damn, I sure wished you lived in Denver, Doris!"

She reached down between them. "Don't ask me to go there with you, then," she sighed. "I might be tempted, and I got a business to run. Speaking of business, this love tool feels about ready to give me the business again. So can we cut out the mush and just screw some more, damn it?"

They could and they did. Doris didn't go in for athletic positions. She just liked old-fashioned screwing, done with athletic skill. He could tell from the way she moved her hot hips that he probably wasn't the only passing stranger she'd entertained this way in recent memory. But that was fair. He knew he was supposed to wake up any minute now. A man having a dream this nice always woke up just before he got to come.

But then he was coming in her, hard and deep, with her soft palms against his bare buttocks to help as she rose to meet his thrusts, softly murmuring, "Oh, yes, yes, that's so nice, Custis."

And damned if she wasn't still there when they came back to their senses, smiling at one another in the soft light. She ran her hands up his bare back to haul him down for a sweet kiss. Then she said matter-of-factly, "If there's more where that came from, let's move it some more. If you've had enough, let's get it out before I get hot again. Either way, we ought to catch some sleep if we intend to get up for work in the morning."

He kissed her again and rolled off, saying, "I'm undecided. But I know you have a business to run. What time do you open, Doris?"

"Nine or so. It depends on how alive it is outside. I have to swamp out before I open, though. You may not buy this, but I'm sort of clean by nature."

He said he'd noticed that and said he'd give her a hand in the morning. "I don't need help if you've got important business to attend to, dear," she said. "You haven't told me what you had to do, come daylight."

He patted her fondly. "I know. That's one of the other things I like about you. But it ain't no secret. Aside from the navy nonsense I told you about, I got to check the Western Union to see if my office wired further instructions or if they can offer any suggestions about another mystery." He told her about the gem stones he couldn't account for, since he doubted she could have slipped them in his pocket aboard a steamer and he'd found in the past that nobody understood the female mind like another female.

When he'd finished, she said, "I think that sassy Russian gal or mayhaps some other crook meant to use you as a distraction, dear. You wasn't supposed to walk off the *Sitka Sally* with the fake rubies. You was supposed to get caught going through naval Customs. Then, while you raised pure hell as the innocent dupe you were supposed to be, somebody would have been able to slip something more valuable past all the confusion, see?"

He snuggled her closer. "Already thought of that. But they never searched me. They searched the princess and all they found on her was a mess of vodka, paid for in Seattle. Of course, it could have been some *other* rascal. It's true they spent more time pawing through a pretty gal's silk underdrawers than on any of the other luggage."

Doris toyed thoughtfully with the hair on his chest as she mused aloud, "I still suspect that Russian bitch. If she was on the up and up, why did she go to so much trouble to seduce a federal agent just before the boat docked?"

He began to play with her chest, too, as he replied. "Maybe she had other reasons. Is there anything in the constitution saying only you get to take advantage of poor weak-willed peace officers?"

"We'll find out how weak you are if you don't let go. I'll allow she might have just enjoyed screwing. But if all she was was a warm-natured woman, how come she gave you a fake name?"

"I've pondered that some, too. She could be a married gal, or she could have something else to hide. She did hold out most of the way up the coast. Maybe when she decided on some what-the-hell she lied about who she might be lest I kiss and tell?"

"Shoot, Custis, this town's small enough to spit across when the wind is with you. How long would it take gossip to get around about a married-up gal, a Russian one at that, with such a warm nature?"

"Don't know. That's what I mean to gossip about in the morning and see if I can find out who she might really be. Whoever she is, I mean to have a word or two with her about them play-pretties in my pocket."

"Oh? And just what else do you mean to discuss with her, dear?" Doris teased.

"I just mean to question her about my suspicions. I'm in a suspicious business."

"What if she turns out to be innocent—of smuggling, I mean? I'll bet you do like her as well as me, don't you?"

He laughed and said, "To tell you the honest truth, I can't recall what she was like right now. Ain't it funny how the one at hand always seems nicer than any you might have noticed in the past?"

She gripped his semi-erection harder and began to stroke it back to life as she said objectively, "I can't recall ever having met a cock as nice as this one, now that you mention it. Would you like to put it in me again or would you rather I Frenched it for you?"

Longarm said he'd like both. So that's just what he got. And she said she liked the way his moustache tickled her, too.

Longarm didn't get to help Doris open up the next morning. She left him sleeping and went down to do it herself. When he finally woke up it was nearly ten and he felt so good he was sorry she wasn't there to help him celebrate. That was the best thing about field work. A man didn't have to worry about the banjo clock on Billy Vail's wall, even if he had to worry more about getting shot.

He slipped the spare key she'd left him in his pocket and went down the back stairs to slip out the back way as Doris served beer to early customers. She was looking mighty chipper this morning, they said.

Since level grades were hard to come by in Sitka the alleyway running behind the storefronts on the main drag was narrow, twisty, and muddy. He could see it was intended more for garbage and dead cats than walking. But he wanted to get clear of the saloon before he cut back to more sensible striding. Aside from his new friend's reputation, the less others knew about where he might be staying the better.

He hadn't gone far when the hairs on the back of his neck told him he might have made a wrong move. But when he turned quickly he didn't see anybody following him. Not close, anyway. The alley twisted so between shingle walls and gray plank fencing that the alley was a perfect setup for an ambush.

He tried to use the same advantage by walking innocently around a bend and turning to wait and see. He thought he might have heard the squish of someone stepping in mud around the bend. But he got tired of waiting, stuck his head back out, and saw nobody squishing anything. He shrugged and moved on faster to get out of such close surroundings. So as he whipped around the corner of a building he was as surprised to see the Indian gal as she was to see him, although she screamed louder.

He stopped, ticked the brim of his hat at her, and told her not to fuss so, adding, "I come in peace, miss. I'm sorry I startled you."

She stared at him like a cornered coyote from behind the trash barrels she'd been rummaging through. She was a pretty little thing of fourteen or so. But her Mother-Hubbard was stained and ragged and her scared moon face could have used some soap was well. She licked her lips and said, "I am not a bad person. I have not been stealing from the white eyes. I only search for things they have no use for. I am not a thief. Please don't take me to jail."

He said, "Nobody's fixing to put you in jail, miss. Rag-picking ain't a federal offense. I don't see how it could even be a town ordinance, do you?"

She sighed. "They said they would put me in jail if I did not stay out of this alley. But it's not fair. Hear me, the white eyes throw things away as useless, then they say we are bad if we want the trash of the white eyes. Please don't tell them you saw me back here. I will let you screw me if you don't tell on me."

Longarm shook his head. "I don't know the local views on rag-picking, but child molesting can't be lawful, miss. I'll tell you what we'd best do. I'll give you . . . oh, fifty cents, and then you'll go somewhere else to play. That way, nobody will have to feel upset."

She frowned up at him. "You will give me half a

dollar? Just to go away?"

"Don't try to figure our mysterious ways, miss. Just take the four bits and git!"

He handed her the silver coin, or tried to. She snatched it from him with a dirty claw and ran like hell back the way he'd just come.

He shrugged and muttered, "She might have said *thanks*, at least. But maybe we forgot to tell her how, poor little critter."

He went on, looking for a way to cut over to the main drag so he could arrive at the naval base with less mud on his boots. He spotted a narrow slit and was about to see if he could fit through it when he heard more footsteps coming fast, and casually drew his .44.

It was Killer Whale. Worse yet, the big Tlingit was sober. He ran up to Longarm, scowling, and stopped in a sort of wrestler's crouch, staring wary-eyed into Longarm's cold smile.

Longarm said, "Look, Chief, this is getting mighty tedious. Big Stink warned me not to kill you. But as you see, I got the drop on you. So if you ain't ready to drop this foolishness, I'll just have to take you to the white eyes' brig and have them keep you on ice till I'm long gone. I ain't got time for kid games."

"I don't know if I want to fight you or not right now," Killer Whale said. "You just gave one of our young girls money. Why? She says you did not even touch her. I know she is very dirty. Her people are no good. But when other white eyes give her money they still want to screw her. I just don't understand you at all, Longarm."

Longarm shrugged and said, "I told her not to try, either. It ain't your fault and it ain't my fault, Killer Whale. Your kind and mine have trouble understanding one another."

"Try me. I am not an ignorant person. I speak English. I know who Jesus is. I know what money is. You just gave that girl as much as a white-eyed woman gives one of our women for a week's housework. Yet you asked nothing of her, nothing."

"Oh, hell, try it this way, Killer Whale. I figured she wouldn't be able to salvage fifty cents' worth of bottles and such back here in a day, and she looked sort of hungry."

"Of course she was hungry. I told you her people were no good. Her mother sells herself to your kind for pennies and her father takes the money to get drunk. But why should you care about the child of no-good Indians?"

"It ain't her fault her folks don't take better care of her. But *somebody* ought to. She said she'd been warned by the law to stay out of this alley. I just gave her some eating money to get rid of her. Why are you making such a big deal out of it?"

"I am trying to understand. You are a lawman and it is true the law forbids our children from even playing in this alley. I am not supposed to be here either. I think they think I would rape a white-eyed woman in her own back yard if I got the chance. Yet you gave the girl money instead of arresting her. Don't you enforce the laws of your own kind?"

"Not when they're just pure silly. We got us a mess of Arapaho living smack inside the Denver city limits, and they don't rape white gals all that much. Is there any point to this discussion, Killer Whale? If you don't want to fight, I got other business to attend."

Killer Whale scratched his jaw and said, "I did want to fight you. I have been following you, hoping to get the jump on you because I don't have a gun. Now I am not so sure. Now I think you must be a good person.

What you did for that girl was good. I am ashamed that I have never thought to give her money, even when I had it. I don't screw dirty little girls, either. But it never occurred to me to give her money. What do you call that in your own language?"

"Charity. I thought you said you were a mission Indian. Didn't them Russian missionaries ever mention Christian charity to you?"

Killer Whale shrugged and said, "I don't know. I was young when you Yankees bought this place from the Little Father. So I didn't have to go to the mission school any more. I mostly remember a place called Hell, where bad Indians go when they die, or so the Russians said. I think they are full of shit. Everyone knows dead people go to meet Raven, whether they've been good or bad. But I think I like this charity totem of yours, Longarm. I think I don't want to fight with you after all. Do you have any enemies we can fight together? Hear me, I am one fighting son of a bitch. Ask anybody, red or white."

Longarm laughed and said he'd think on it. He held out his hand to part friendly, once he'd put his gun away. The big Indian took it gingerly. Then he grinned ear to ear. "We are friends, now?" he asked.

Longarm said that was about the size of it and ducked into the slot. He scraped some getting out to the main drag, but he made it. He knew, after he had breakfast at a nearby beanery, that he'd never get back through that slot again now. Not knowing when he'd get as good a chance to eat again, he put away an extra slice of apple pie on top of his steak and eggs.

Chapter 6

There was a different guard on duty at the naval base. Better yet, he had instructions to show Longarm through with an apology for the night before. When Longarm got to the officers' club the same duty officer who should have been called the night before was waiting to buy him a drink and apologize some more. He said, "That stupid kid is in the brig awaiting my pleasure, Longarm. You were gone by the time he told me about it as I was making my rounds. I swear good help is hard to find these days. Will you be content with a masthead and thirty days for the idiot?"

Longarm shook his head. "If it's for me to say, I'd rather you turned him loose. He was only trying to do his duty as the good Lord gave him the brains to do it with."

"By God, that's very generous of you, Longarm. We both know the boy should have let you through!"

"Did he have orders to that effect, Lieutenant?"

"Not as such. But the whole base knows who you are and that you're here on navy business. I don't know what could have gotten into that poor fool last night."

Longarm told the enlisted barkeep to make his rye if they had it. "I do," he said. "I was a green buck-ass private one time. He was scared. He was trained not to question orders and he had orders to keep anyone but an officer or a seaman with a pass from passing through that gate. So that's what he done. I'll confess I was a mite vexed about it at the time, but since my evening in town ended more pleasant than I want to go into, I ain't mad at all at the kid right now."

The j.g. smiled and said, "Well, a day in the brig will teach him to use his head next time. What was it you wanted last night, anyway?" he added.

"I *thought* I wanted to bed down in your B.O.Q. Now I don't. I come over this morning to see how soon you'll be holding that court-martial, so I can get the hell out of here."

The j.g. picked up his own glass, clinked it against Longarm's, and said, "Now that Seaman Lee's dug such a deep grave for himself he faces a full court-martial and we have to wait for a rear admiral to make up the board. Don't worry. He's due in any minute. His gun boat was just up near Attu, chasing seal pirates."

"Oh, Lord, you got *pirates* up here too?"

"If they're not U. S. citizens and they're sealing in Alaskan waters, you can bet your ass they're pirates. Uncle Sam paid over seven million dollars for this territory and, so far, the returns on his investment have been dismal."

Longarm shrugged and said, "Let's talk about my return to the States. I still don't see why on earth you need me to try a deserter I never saw before yesterday. You'd already arrested him long before I got here. So what in thunder could I testify about? I told you he wasn't the real Soapy Smith."

The j.g. nodded. "That's what the admiral will want to hear, Longarm. The asshole in the brig is still protesting that he's Soapy Smith, not the Seaman Lee we have on the books as a deserter. We don't have a photograph of the real Soapy Smith. Some people here in Sitka say Lee does look a lot like Soapy Smith and the defense team will be duty-bound to produce any witnesses willing to swear Lee *could* be Soapy Smith. So, to convict beyond the shadow of a doubt..."

"Yeah, yeah. You need someone who knows Soapy Smith personal, if you have to be picky about it. But, look here, old Lee don't have the scar I left on the mortal hide of the real Soapy Smith. Don't that count for something?"

The j.g. shook his head. "Not when you have a good defense team and a lot of brass. Lee says he was only pinked by your bullet in that Denver gunfight. Our medical officer says it's possible for a minor wound to heal without a scar, so—"

"Minor wound my ass," Longarm cut in. "I blowed the son of a bitch flat on his ass with a .44-40 slug in him. Not long enough ago for even a .22 scar to heal entire."

"Was there any medical record we could produce? Did you take the real Soapy Smith to a hospital in Denver after you shot him?"

"Hell, he wasn't shot *that* serious. I just told him to leave town on the next train, and he must have. For I promised I'd kill him all the way next time I saw his face in Denver. Last I heard, he was still alive. Up here in Alaska, as a matter of fact."

The j.g. slid his empty glass to the barkeep for another and morosely observed, "Swell. In other words, the real Soapy Smith had been established as a shady resident of Alaska Territory and that man in the brig who looks like him doesn't have to produce a bullet scar if there's no official record either one of them was ever shot by you."

"Well, hell, I don't care if they want to say I never shot old Soapy Smith. I never said I shot him *serious*."

"Nevertheless, you do know the real Soapy Smith on sight. Ergo, you can testify whether the accused is him or not. Ergo, they want you to testify, and the admiral ought to be here within the week. Certainly by next week at the latest."

Longarm slid his empty shotglass back for more and said, "We're starting to talk in circles. Let's talk more sensible. Is it safe for me to assume you navy gents are running everything federal up here, from Indian Affairs to Customs?"

The j.g. nodded. "Of course, since no territorial government's been set up by Washington as yet. We allow the civilian settlements to elect their own town constabularies. But the U. S. Navy runs all serious government services except the U. S. Mail. Why do you ask?"

"You ain't running Indian Affairs worth shit. But let's not worry about that just yet. I got a Customs problem. Can you think of anything one could buy in the United States, in Seattle, that would be unlawful to smuggle into Alaska?"

The j.g. frowned thoughtfully and replied, "Not offhand. If a product was U. S. made no customs would be due on it in a U. S. territory. If it had already been imported into the country, any duties would have already been paid, no?"

"That's the way I see it. I still think someone might have acted smugglesome on us. My steamer stopped a few times in British Columbia. What sort of contraband do you boys catch coming out of Canada?"

The j.g. shook his head and said, "We don't. In the first place, there are few British products subject to heavy duties. In the second place, there's no way of controlling trade between Canada and the U. S. even when you know where the border might be. Whites as well as Indians drift back and forth across the long unguarded border between Alaska and the Northwest Territories of Canada. What kind of contraband are we talking about, Long-arm?"

Longarm stared down at his fresh drink thoughtfully. "If I knew, we wouldn't be talking about it. It can't be booze or guns whether you want the Indians to have either or not. Such bulky stuff would be safer to smuggle over the mountains than through a mess of officers standing on a dock. I had jewels or perhaps gold in mind. Prices are mighty high up here. Wouldn't gold and jewels sell for more in Alaska?"

"Forget gold. There's no Customs duty on gold. Anyone's allowed to carry gold coins issued by any country through Customs. Aside from that, the price of gold is regulated by the U. S. Treasury. So gold is gold in any U. S. territory."

"What about going the other way? Suppose I smuggled gold into Alaska, said I found it up here in a creek, and snuck it over the hills into Canada?"

"You'd sure get a lot of exercise. The U. S. and the British Empire are on the same international gold standard. What was that other idea, about jewelry?"

"Suppose I had some diamonds, rubies, or whatever, and I figured Alaska gals would pay more for 'em than

I could get in the States?"

"Did you buy the play-pretties in the States?"

"Bought 'em or stole 'em. What difference do it make?"

"It won't work. Jewelry coming from the U. S. to the U. S. just isn't subject to import duty. Hell, Longarm, half the women getting off that boat had some jewelry on. We don't question them about their corsets or hatpins, either."

"Not even if they got on in Canadian waters?"

"I suppose we could. But we don't."

"Then what in thunder *were* you looking for as you made us all go through that?"

The j.g. took a sip and said, "Liquor without revenue seals. Guns we'd like to register in case someone peddles them to a Tlingit. That sort of thing. Frankly, it's just a formality. We've yet to catch anyone smuggling anything into Alaska. But Washington expects us to go through the motions."

Longarm looked disgusted and said, "Thank the Lord the Post Office is still delivering the mail. I'm sure you boys up here are all set if the Manchu Empire decides to invade. But I don't see what else you could be doing here."

"Come now, we have to protect the natural resources and keep the Indians under control."

"Yeah, I'm sure the seals feel safer, knowing nobody but us is allowed to skin 'em, and I just met an Indian you was controlling so good she was eating garbage. By the way, did you know some of the local whites has been screwing Tlingit gals?"

The j.g. shrugged. "That's hardly a U.S. Navy matter. Is it our fault the savages have no morals?"

"I ain't talking about immoral Indians. I'm talking about whites molesting wards of the U. S. government.

76

Didn't you know it's against federal law to exploit Indians sexual? That's what giving a kid a few cents for a screw is called, exploiting."

"Oh, hell, Longarm, would you rather have our roughnecks just rape them, without even offering to pay?"

"That would sure simplify things. You could arrest 'em for sure for rape. Look, I ain't saying it's wrong entirely for red and white to enjoy one another's company. I'll confess I've bent the rules a few times myself. But it ain't sensible to let things like that get out of hand and ugly. Half the trouble between our breed and others has been occasioned by the fact us whites are so willing to screw the wife or daughter of a man we don't find fit to drink with. You've let the town law pass an ordinance saying Tlingit ain't allowed to walk the streets where more fashionable white whores can. Yet you allow whites too cheap to pay a white whore to mess with Indian gals. Can't you see how that looks to an already sort of surly Indian?"

He could tell by the look in the other man's eyes the lieutenant couldn't. So he finished his drink and said he'd best move on down the road. The lieutenant asked if he didn't mean to wait until the base commander showed up. Longarm said he'd already jawed more than he'd wanted to about Soapy Smith and other tedious matters.

He left the officers' club and headed back to town. As he strode along the cinder path a ragged-ass Tlingit kid cut him off to say, "Brothers from mission send me to find you, Longarm."

The tall deputy smiled down and replied, "You found me, pard. How did you know who I was?"

The kid said, "You are Longarm because you look like Longarm. The real people have been talking about you. Come. I will show you the way."

"I know where the mission is, son," said Longarm.

But the Indian kid said, "We are not going there. Brother Boris said you are looking for a bad white-eyed woman. She is staying at a farm the Russians abandoned when most of them went away years ago."

"Are you sure the Princess Tasha is hiding out on some old Russian homestead?"

"I do not know her name. She is white of skin and black of hair. She has bigger tits than our women. Brother Boris said to show you where she is and that you would know what to do to her."

The Indian led him off the path and through a mess of blackberry bushes. Then they were in second-growth timber and Longarm looked back wistfully on his experience with the sticker brush.

The virgin forest around Sitka had been logged rough-and-ready so that long dead and now rotten logs of considerable size lay in wait no matter which way one tried to figure a path through the skinny, close-set second growth. The logs left because they had turned out to be too heavy to skid or perhaps because they split on falling were too big around to step over easily and so rotten that when one put a boot on one to climb over, they turned to soggy punk and tried to suck a man's boots off. The short, wiry Tlingit moved through the tanglewood as if he'd been born there, which he probably had. He let the damp branches whip back in Longarm's face as he plowed through. Longarm couldn't cuss him. There was no other way to move through second growth. The damned branches grew out from the skinny trunks to brush tips with one another. The only thing that kept Longarm from getting lost within a quarter of a mile of town was the slope of the ground and the way the overhead clouds kept moving from west to east.

They went over a ridge. The only way Longarm could tell was by the way they were going downhill after going uphill a spell. He couldn't see ten yards ahead or, come to think of it, back or sideways. He was tempted to tell the Indian kid to slow down. But he just held his left elbow up to block most of the punches the woods kept throwing at his face. He made sure he didn't lose sight of his guide. As soft and soggy as the forest ground was, neither made any sound with their feet. They came to a rivulet of running water, jumped across, and went over another ridge. Then his guide swung to the north and stopped. Longarm couldn't see why. Then he heard the sound of a hoe or pick crunching into gravel soil somewhere off in the woods.

The Indian kid said, "We are almost there. She is digging. What do you think she could be digging, Longarm?"

"Don't know. Let's go see. Is she alone?" Longarm asked.

"She was a few minutes ago. I do not think she wants anyone to know she is there. She has no smoke rising from her chimney. If she is Russian, she is evil. She did not go to Mass this morning. If she is not Russian, she is still evil. She would have no business on an old Russian farm if she was not Russian. Be careful, Longarm. She has a gun."

Longarm took the lead. He came to a mossy stone wall. If what lay on the far side was the remains of an abandoned farm, the woods didn't know it. The old field had gone to saplings. But they did seem a might thinner, and of course there were no big logs to worry about as he strode toward the sound of digging.

He spotted movement ahead and moved closer. It was Tasha, sure as shooting. She had changed into blue jeans and a smock-like gray cossack's shirt. Her hair was pinned up and tucked under a red kerchief. She had an S&W on one trim hip and a miner's pick in her dainty hands. Behind her, the silvery logs of an old tumbledown cabin outlined her toil as she stood shin-deep in the hole she had dug so far. Longarm stepped out into the little pool of grass around the cabin and said howdy. Tasha screamed and dropped her pick. But she saw who it was before she slapped leather and must have decided they were still pals.

She said, "Custis, what on earth are you doing here?"

"I was about to ask you the same thing. Did you know you forgot your accent when you was coming or otherwise surprised?"

She said, *"Mais non."* Then she laughed sheepishly. "All right, I may have grown up in Portland, but I am a Russian. Or at least my parents were. They moved down to the states when Alaska was sold. This used to be our family farm."

"Mighty small spread for a Baranov, ain't it?"

"All right, so my name's really Natasha Rostov. But we did have money. My folks were in the sea-otter trade and you've no idea how much a Chinese Mandarin will pay for sea-otter fur."

"Is that what you're digging for? No offense, but you're more likely to run into a gopher than a sea otter at the rate you're going."

She looked around and asked, "Are we alone, Custis?"

"Ain't sure," he told her. "Don't take your duds off just yet, honey. We got more important matters to discuss right now. For openers, I got your red garnets any time you'd like 'em back. I just found out you could have wore 'em ashore bold as brass. So there was no need for you to hide 'em on me after all."

She looked sincerely confused. "What on earth are you talking about? I didn't give you any garnets to keep for me, dear. I don't even *like* garnets. They're so working-class."

"What are you working at, then? You ought to have at least a pan and some running water if you aim to start a gold rush."

"Let's go inside. I can see you'll never be satisfied until I . . . well . . . satisfy you."

He looked around to see how his Indian guide was taking all this. He didn't see the kid. He doubted the Tlingit had taken off, though.

He followed Tasha inside the cabin. It was hard to tell they were inside anything. The roof sure could have used some new shingles. But she had a waterproof tarp thrown over the bedroll under the more solid part of the roof. As she started to slip off the smock he said, "Hold on now. You know I'm only human. But right now I'm on duty. You got a lot of answering to do, Miss Rostov, and we've already established how you screw."

She turned to face him, gun on hip and naked from the waist up, to call him a brute.

"I'm in a brutal business, honey. So let's start from the beginning and tell it true this time," he demanded.

She shrugged her bare shoulders, bouncing her bare breasts in a mighty interesting way. "All right. I didn't know who you were, at first, but I could see you looked armed and dangerous. By the time I was sure you were a lawman I'd already told a few fibs and . . . well, I didn't want you to stop, and I knew you would, if I changed my tale."

"Never mind why you lied to me. Tell me what the hell's going on *now*."

"I'm searching for buried treasure. Don't laugh. It's

the truth. My late father wasn't exactly the governor of Russian Alaska. He was, as I said, a Russian trader. The Tsar was so greedy about other people's profits..."

"Meaning your old man might have held out on the Little Father's tax collectors?"

"There's no 'might' about it, Custis. I was raised on the story. I told you my family traded mostly with the Manchu Empire. Expensive otter pelts were traded in China for money that had to be declared and diamonds that were easy to smuggle out a few at a time. In time, my father amassed quite a fortune in diamonds, meaning to move to your country eventually, where there is no income tax and an honest merchant is allowed to spend his hard-earned money on himself and his family instead of these degenerates in Petrograd."

"Never mind the political lectures, either. You sure do like to go the long way around a simple story, Tasha. Your old man got his hands on a mess of diamonds. Then what?"

"You people bought Alaska. It was all so sudden. We weren't ready for it. My father had buried the diamonds out here for safekeeping. But we actually had some tenant Indians farming the place, to look innocent. We lived in town, in a more imposing house."

"How did your father get to be *we?* Was you in on it or not?"

"Silly! I was only a child. I barely remember my early life here in Sitka and of course I was never out to this tenant farm as a wee one. You're mixing me up to trip me up, aren't you?"

"Yep. Keep talking. You folk just had Alaska sold out from under you. Then what?"

She shrugged again. He wondered if she knew what that did to his glands. He decided she must. She said,

"My father was confused and frightened. He decided it would be safer to leave his treasure where it was for the time being. He decided right. The Russian secret police caught one trader trying to leave with more gold than he'd declared and nobody ever heard from him again. We took a boat bound for Russia via the American West Coast. We got off in Oregon. My father had of course been allowed to take some money out, so he was able to set up in Portland as a furrier. We lived quite well, as a matter of fact. I guess that was why my father kept putting off going back for his diamonds once things calmed down under American rule. He kept saying he was going to, but meanwhile his new business kept him tied up. He came down with consumption and had to put it off until he was well enough to travel. Naturally, by this time I knew the whole story. But he never told me exactly where he'd buried his wealth, save for the fact it was somewhere around this cabin. I offered, more than once, to come up here myself and get it. He said it was too dangerous for a mere girl. A few months ago he died. After we settled his estate and I found myself with a little money and freedom, I decided it was time to reclaim the family fortune. That's all there is to it, dear."

She unbuckled her gun rig and set it aside to unbutton her jeans. "Hold the thought," he said. "You still left a few things out. Aboard the boat you made me promise not to look you up once we got here. As you can see, I just broke that promise. I'm waiting to hear how come you asked it, Tasha."

She slid the jeans down, sighed, and said, "For one thing, I knew I'd get little work done if you were around. For another, I simply didn't want anyone to know what I was really up here for."

She moved gracefully over to the bedroll and sank to

the canvas with an expectant expression on her still possibly fibbing face. He stayed put and ignored the tingle in his pants. "Let's try her another way. Dug-up Russian diamonds might not enter the U. S. duty free. So why should a pretty gal pester a U. S. federal agent about whether she might be going to back to Seattle with a fortune in diamonds or not?"

"How could gem stones dug from U. S. soil be subject to U. S. Customs, dear?" she asked.

He studied on that before he said, "I ain't sure. Alaska is U. S. now. But it wasn't then, and . . . Hell, that's for lawyers to worry about. You do mean to report any jewelry you find to the law as part of your late father's estate, don't you?"

She sighed. "I suppose I'd better, now. I'm not sure I could trust you not to turn a friend in, even a good friend, you mean old thing."

Longarm chuckled fondly. "I knew you'd figure out why they hung a badge on me, sooner or later. I don't see anything too unlawful about what you've done so far. You just make sure you mention the diamonds to the government when and if you find 'em and we'll say no more about it."

He turned to leave. Tasha gasped, "Custis, where do you think you're going?"

He said, "Ain't *thinking*. I *know*. If you wasn't the one who flimflammed me with them other gem stones, I still have to catch up with whoever it *was*. So I'm going back to town, of course."

"Just like that? Leaving me in this ridiculous position and condition? Why do you think I just got undressed, you idiot?"

"Well, you *was* working hot and sweaty just now."

84

She laughed incredulously and insisted, "Come back here and treat me right, you brute! I thought we were lovers. You can't just walk away from me now!"

He turned in the doorway and said, "You're still fibbing to me at both ends, Tasha. So we ain't friends no more."

He turned to go. She leaped up and chased him out the door, pleading, "Come back inside, damn it! I swear I've told you all there is to tell!"

He turned to face her. She sure looked tempting as the sun burst through the clouds to dapple her naked hide in trembling shadows from the overhead spruce branches. He said, "You told me a sad tale about a loving daughter living with her family till the day she could get back to the old homestead to dig for whatever. You left some things out. Like how you learned to screw so good as well as free and easy."

She blushed all over and lowered her eyes to stammer, "Can't a girl keep *any* secrets from you? All right. I never said I was a virgin and I'll admit I practically raped you aboard that steamer. I've been married, twice, and maybe I've had a few lovers as well. Satisfied?"

He shrugged and said, "Not yet. I mean to wire Portland and see if a furrier called Rostov died there recent."

She sobbed, covered her face with her hands, and ran back into the cabin. He watched her receding bare and wistfully, shrugged, and walked into the trees.

The Tlingit kid popped into sight nearby, grinning.

"You can show me how to get to town from here," Longarm said. "Tell your people I don't want nobody messing with that white gal, and I mean it."

The Indian boy laughed. "You must be made of iron. She looks even better with her clothes off and you turned

85

her down! Oh, what a good story to tell! How did you get to be so strong, Longarm?"

The white man shrugged. "It ain't easy."

Chapter 7

By the time the Tlingit kid led him back to town and vanished into thin air, Longarm was wondering what was wrong with him that morning. For he'd passed up a perfectly good woman and Doris wouldn't be available until late that night. Meanwhile it wasn't much past noon, yet, and he didn't have another important thing to do until he helped Doris with those heavy shutters.

He went to the Western Union office. It was better than just standing around watching smelly gents in gumboots walk by. But the wire from Billy Vail was as tedious as he had expected. The office instructed him to just do as the infernal navy told him to do, for now. Vail added that the real Soapy Smith had last been seen in some Alaska fishing village called Skagway, dealing suspicious cards. The clerk said Skagway was way the hell up the Inland Passage, and card-sharping wasn't a federal offense, so what the hell.

He wired the Portland county clerk to see if any death certificates made out under the name of Rostov had been recorded in the past ten years, giving Tasha plenty of rope.

He considered wiring the Portland board of education to see if any little gal by her name had ever gone to school there. But that could be more trouble than it was worth, so he dropped the notion. She could always say she had gone to some private or religious school. She likely would whether she had or not. She hadn't said what married names she might have used in the past, or where she'd been married, so there was no sense pestering justices of the peace all over the States. There was nothing to do about her now but to wait for the wire from Portland and see if she came running into town with a sack of diamonds.

He saw the assay office ahead and that reminded him of the flimflammed garnets and other jewelry questions he ought to check out.

He went in and found the blonde still grinding the same ore sample or more likely another. She looked up and brightened when she saw who it was. She said. "I was hoping you'd drop by. Something odd just happened."

"How odd, Kathleen?" he asked, leaning on the far side of her counter. "Two men were in about an hour ago, asking about garnets," she said.

"Do tell? I hope you didn't mention the ones I left in your safekeeping, Kathleen."

"Do I look that foolish? I didn't even mention your name. I just played dumb."

He nodded. "Sometimes that's the smartest thing one can do. But if they wasn't after my garnets, whose garnets were they after?"

"They asked if I had any for sale," she said. "I do have some garnet rings in the case, of course. But they said they were looking for red garnets. The ones that look something like rubies."

"I'll bet they were. What did they look like, Kathleen?"

"One was dressed sort of nice, like you, only his suit was black. His Stetson was black, too. He was smooth-shaven. The other looked more like a logger. Dark checked wool jacket and a knit cap like loggers wear. They were both packing pistols. I don't mind telling you I was a little nervous until the nicer-looking one assured me they wanted to *buy* jewelry instead of getting it the other way."

Longarm frowned thoughtfully.

"What do you suppose they really had in mind, Custis?" Kathleen asked.

He said, "Don't know. They ain't here to ask. You sure my name wasn't mentioned even once?"

She shook her head. "I thought that could be what they were fishing for, so I listened sharp. They never. They just looked over the few garnets we have for sale, asked if I didn't have any others to show them, and when I assured them I didn't, thanked me and left. Oh, Custis, I was so scared. I'm still scared. I think I'd best just close up shop and wait until my father comes back."

He shrugged. "It's a free country, but a poor way to do business. What's that ore you're grinding, chloride?"

She dimpled. "The prospector who brought it in thought it might be. Alaska Territory is a big tease. There are signs of color all up and down the coast ranges, but so far nobody's ever made a lucky strike. I hear that over in the Yukon . . ."

"Let's not talk about mayhaps and far away," he said. "I need a jeweler's educated guesses on gem stones that might turn out to be closer than the Yukon. If I brought you a diamond, would you know it from busted glass, Kathleen?"

She looked hurt and replied, "What a mean thing to say! Of course I'd be able to tell if a diamond was real or not. That's easy. You can fool us on some semi-precious stones, but diamonds don't look like anything else if you know this business, and I do."

"So far so good. Diamonds are worth more than any other kind of rocks, right?" She nodded and he went on, "So if I wanted to convert a fortune into diamonds, how much poundage would I be talking about, Kathleen?"

She blinked and replied, "Good heavens, an *ounce* of diamonds could ransom a rajah, Custis. Some first color stones alone are worth a million."

"I give up. What's first color?"

"Oh, diamonds are graded by color and freedom from flaws, with the flaws more important, since some women fancy a bit of color in a good stone. The absolute top-quality diamond is as colorless as pure water. They all have some flaws under magnification. That's what makes it so easy to spot a real one from a fake. One flaw you never spot in a diamond is a bubble. They only crack a certain way. Sometimes you spy a tiny bit of carbon black and—"

He halted her with a wave of his hand and said, "I ain't fixing to *buy* one, Kathleen. So what you're saying is that a gent could leave a mighty small poke of diamonds buried somewhere and it'd still add up to a lot of *dinero?*"

"Heavens, yes. One or two good stones could be worth almost any amount you'd like to guess at. It would depend on the brilliance and cut, of course. The run-of-the-mill diamonds you see for sale wouldn't be as . . .

Wait a minute; I'll show you."

She reached under the counter and produced a heavy gold ring with a bitty glitter set in it. She handed it to him. "This ring sells for two hundred dollars," she told him. "The gold is fourteen-karat. The chip diamond is poor quality, but it's real."

He held the flashy gambler's ring up to the light and turned it to make it flash more. "Well, if you say so, it's a diamond," he said. "I could pack an awful lot of stones this size in a vest pocket and never notice. Suppose I did. What would, say, a pocketful of bitty diamonds like this be worth?"

She shook her head. "It's not that simple. Each stone would have its own price and that could vary a great deal. But even if we're talking about bort, a pocketful would be worth close to a thousand, I suppose."

"Bort?"

"That's what we call almost useless diamonds. It's a South African term. No diamond is *completely* worthless. Even the *black* bort they sort in South Africa is valuable for cutting and grinding. I'll bet you can't guess what diamond dust is used to cut."

"Sure I can. Other diamonds. I read, some, when there's nothing better to do. I doubt if the diamonds I may want you to look at for me later could be sandpaper quality. You've convinced me even a handful of low-quality diamonds would be worth a trip to Alaska. Now if only I could figure out why someone wanted to smuggle garnets *into* Alaska . . . But I can't, and I see you're busy, so . . ."

She asked him not to leave and came around the counter to dash past him to the front door. She hung the CLOSED sign in the window and pulled down the shade. It felt a lot darker in there now as she said, "I'm scared. Do you really have to go so soon?"

He didn't. On the other hand, he was already feeling horny enough, and if he was reading the smoke signals in her otherwise innocent eyes wrong it was going to hurt like hell. He said, "Well, I didn't bring my checkerboard. What else do you do to pass the time in here when you ain't open for business? It's sure too dark to read."

She moved closer, flirting with his boot tops with the swishing of her skirts, and sighed. "I know. But I'm sure we'll think of something."

He either had to grab her or let her push him through the glass counter she'd trapped him against. As he took her in his arms he murmured, "When did you say you figured on your old man getting back, honey?"

She turned her face up to him, eyes closed, and answered in a dreamy voice. "He won't be back for days, dear. Both the front and back doors lock from the inside, in case of burglars. So there's no way even *he* could get in, unless we *let* him in."

He kissed her. She not only kissed back but seemed to be trying to screw him standing up, with all their fool clothes in the way. So when they came up for air he laughed and said, "All right. One condition. I want your word as a pal that you didn't make up that story about mysterious strangers in the market for mysterious garnets."

She thrust her trim hips against him teasingly as she asked, "Why, Custis, why would I make a thing like that up?"

"To have an excuse for closing so early, for openers. You've no idea how often women has fibbed to me in the past just to trap me alone in the dark."

She laughed, took his hand, and said, "Let's talk about it in the back, where it's even darker." But as she led him to his doom she added reassuringly, "Those men were really here before, bless them. I was wondering how on earth I'd ever get to know you better."

They got to know one another quite well once Kathleen had him on the cot in the back workshop. She explained that while the bed in her quarters upstairs might be softer, she was in too great a hurry and liked a firm foundation under her in any case.

He liked the results, too, once they'd stripped down some and he was pounding her bare behind against the taut canvas.

He came faster than usual, thanks partly to Tasha's earlier inspiration but mostly because Kathleen felt so good. She felt his ejaculation, sighed, and then went even crazier when he didn't let her down. She moaned, "Oh, I never dreamed it would be this good, and I dreamed about you all night!"

He closed his eyes and tried to make it last this time as he groaned, "Powder River and let her buck!"

Then, just as they were climaxing together, they heard a heavy pounding on the back door across the room. As they stiffened in mutual surprise a husky male voice called in at them, "Honey? I'm home. Let me in."

Kathleen stared up at Longarm in terror as she gasped, "Oh, my God, it's my husband!"

Longarm started to ask how her father had suddenly turned into her husband, but this was no time for idle chatter. He pulled out of her and yanked his pants up pronto. Then he grabbed the other stuff he'd scattered about in his haste to get in what he now saw was lots of trouble. Meanwhile, Kathleen was shouting, "Coming, dear!" even though she'd just come another way and wasn't about to open that door before she could get her own duds on.

Longarm didn't wait to see the last of it. He moved out front, dressing on the fly and the hell with buttons. He turned the sign in the window around and let the shade whip up before he stepped out the front door as he heard the back door opening. Women never had any consideration about a man's buttons at such times. He heard her delighted voice shout, "Oh, darling, it's so good to have you home!" as he strode off, buttoning his fly under his gun rig and trying not to notice the two women in sunbonnets trying not to notice him. He didn't think he ought to get anywhere near Doris before he'd managed to wash, women being so suspicious by nature. So he swung into the next saloon he came to and asked if they had a gents' room.

The barkeep laughed, pointed, and said, "Don't spill that beer in here, pilgrim!"

Longarm laughed back and headed for the sanitary facilities. Fortunately the place was almost empty and no gals were present. But all but a couple of the others laughed at him, too, as he dashed through the door marked GENTS.

He locked the door behind him, dropped his pants, and washed himself good. The Lord alone knew what an innocent wayfaring stranger could pick up from a woman as cheatsome as that *last* one had been! She hadn't said whether she'd laid the two strangers looking for garnets. But if she hadn't, they sure must have been ugly. Longarm was not given to false modesty. He knew he was a gent some gals admired. But even Doris had made him work harder than that, and poor Doris didn't have a man of her own who'd just stepped out on business.

He stared into the mirror above the sink and muttered, "All right, you dumb bastard. How in thunder are we supposed to get them garnets out of Kathleen's safe without having to fight the husband we just hung a moose rack on?"

His image had no suggestion to offer. He buttoned up and simmered down. He lit a smoke to give himself a more innocent look as he made ready to step out to the applause he felt sure was coming. Gents who drank in mid-afternoon because they had nothing better to do tended to enjoy rough humor and he had dashed in here sort of comically fast.

He shrugged and unlocked the door as he prepared to take a bow to them. Then he blinked and muttered, "Jesus, you really have been thinking with your cock instead of your brains today!"

But Longarm was thinking, now, so even though the two gents waiting outside had their guns out, he surprised the hell out of them by coming out low, gun in hand, to crab to one side as the two of them blew holes through the air at chest level.

Longarm didn't have to worry about other targets. Saloons always cleared fast when moody-looking gents got up to stand outside a door with guns drawn. The barkeep could be anywhere. Longarm didn't care. He fired first at the one in the black suit, since he looked more like a gun for hire. Then he fired into the one in the logger's cap without waiting for the gunslick to hit the floor.

The rougher-looking one went down like a slaughtered lamb. The other son of a bitch was still looming in the gunsmoke. Longarm fired twice and the tougher one staggered back, trying to train his own gun on Longarm while apparently skating backward at the same time.

Longarm put his last revolver round in him, dropped the Colt, and went for his derringer. But then the gunslick crashed through the front window and, from the way one boot heel still hung on the low sill, Longarm figured he had time to reload. So he picked up the .44 and did so as he walked out front to view the damage.

He saw the man in the black suit wasn't in a conversational mood, even though, sure enough, his face went with the Wanted flier Longarm had remembered almost too late. He went back inside. The barkeep was peeping over the top of the bar, wide-eyed. He said, "Jesus Christ! They sure must have wanted to piss mighty bad!"

Longarm ignored him. He kicked the burly man in the plaid jacket to see if he was at all attentive and when the thug spit blood and an unkind remark about his mother up at him, Longarm said, "You ain't got much time to talk. So who the hell might you be?"

The dying man told Longarm to do something that was likely painful, if it would work. Longarm kicked him again and said, "Come on. I know your pal out front is the late Tex Jones, unusual as such a handle might sound. He used to shoot people on demand. You appear to be out of business, too. But if you'll give me your name and address in the States I'll see your kin gets what's in your pockets. Otherwise some townee figures to enjoy your gains, however ill-gotten."

The man at his feet growled, "You just go to hell, Longarm."

Longarm kicked him again. "Cut that out and let me die in peace, you cruel bastard," he groaned. "I don't have to tell you nothing."

"You do if you want to die in peace, pard. I reckon you have a good dozen or more kicks coming before you get to wait for me in Hell. So you can tell me what this was all about, or write your congressman about cruel and unusual punishment for all I care."

He kicked him again, making sure he didn't kick the same busted rib he'd felt with his toe the last time. The wounded man whimpered like a hurt pup and gasped, "I'm Waco Woodford, I ain't got no kin, and you're one mother-fucking son of a bitch in case nobody's told you yet."

A familiar copper badge came in, gun drawn, as Longarm said, pleasantly enough to the hired gun, "What I really want you to tell me is who hired you boys, and why."

"Ask Tex. He was the one as drawed up the contract. He only recruited me when he heard it was *you* that needed shooting, Longarm."

"Tex ain't in condition to talk. You are. So let's see if we can't do better than that."

The town law gasped as Longarm kicked the downed man again. He said, "Longarm, that's pure cruel, what you're doing."

Longarm said, "I know. This son of a bitch was in a cruel line of work. So he's going to tell me more or I aim to treat him cruel as hell. Who hired you and how come you knew about them garnets, Waco?"

Waco didn't answer, even when Longarm kicked him again. He couldn't. Longarm dropped to one knee, felt the greasy side of his throat, and muttered, "Shit, he sure was a sissy for a man in his business."

The town law gulped. "The one out front is deader than a turned-bad goose, too. Did you say there was paper out on these gents?"

Longarm rose, trying not to look disgusted, and said, "The one out front is wanted in more than one state for murder and the family of one victim was so upset they posted a thousand on the son of a bitch. Never heard of this other asshole. But if you want Tex Jones you got to take *him* off my hands, too."

"Hell, for a thousand dollars I'll take a dozen. Who do I wire about the bounty?"

Longarm got out his notebook and wrote down the name of the Montana rancher who would be pleased to learn his son's killer no longer walked the earth, even in Alaska. He tore the sheet out and handed it to the copper badge, not mentioning the odds on collecting, folk being the way they was, once they cooled down and talked to a lawyer about words possibly spoken in haste. Once Sitka took credit for the rascals, Sitka couldn't give them back. That was the first thing so far today that had worked out right. He still didn't know who was sending hired guns his way, or how he was going to reclaim those garnets they'd been sent to get as well.

Chapter 8

When there was no other way to do something, it still had to be done. So once Longarm finished discussing cadavers with the local coroner and wired the result to Denver he marched back up the other way, sucked in his gut, and went into the assay and jewelry establishment of what he now knew was the business of Mr. and Mrs. Snow.

Kathleen was alone out front when he entered. She gaped at him as if he'd been the whole James–Younger gang in the flesh and hissed, "Custis, are you crazy?"

"Nope," he said. "Not even pissed off, now that I'd had time to simmer down. I come to get my jewels."

Before she could answer a skinny gent who looked like he led a hard life, and likely did, came out from the back, smiling politely enough. Kathleen looked like she was looking for a hole in the floor to drop into and Longarm felt stomach muscles tighten, for the gent was

99

packing a sawed-off shotgun.

But he's apparently just been cleaning it, for he put it under the counter as his wife said weakly, "Darling, this is the federal deputy I was telling you about. He came to get those garnets out of our safe."

Snow brightened at Longarm. "By George, I just heard about that gunfight you were in down the way. We heard the shots clear in the back. You must have been having that fight just about the time I . . . ah . . . got home."

Kathleen looked as relieved as Longarm felt. She turned around to drop down in front of the safe. She didn't look half as nice to Longarm, now that he knew how easy she was, but he was a good sport. He smiled back at the poor bastard wedded to the little cheat and allowed she'd helped him a lot already with her knowledge of the jewelry business. Snow said he was sure his little gal knew as much or more than he did. Longarm didn't see fit to argue that point, either.

He said, "I understand you was over on the mainland till just now. You mind if I ask you how you got there and back?"

Snow looked puzzled. "By steam launch, of course. See here, am I under some sort of suspicion, Deputy?"

Longarm shook his head. "Not hardly. We've established where you was the last few days and nights. You couldn't have been plotting against me even if you had a reason. I asked how one gets about up here because I may want to do the same before I'm done. Do you own your own launch?"

Snow shook his head. "No. Some of the fishermen will run you hither and yon, out of salmon season, if you make it worth your while. See old Charly Bluenose down at the docks if you want to hire a launch. He'll tell you where he was with me the last few days as well."

Longarm didn't look at his wife as he told Snow, "I don't play chess when the game's more like checkers, Mr. Snow. I got more likely suspects, if only I knew what I was supposed to suspect them of."

Kathleen rose with the cloth-wrapped garnets. As she handed them to Longarm her husband asked in a natural way if he could have a look at them. Longarm spread the cloth open on the counter. Snow got out a jeweler's glass and held the strand up to the light. He pursed his lips and said, "These aren't garnets, honey lamb. You must have examined them by lamplight, right!"

Kathleen looked worried, as she had every right to. "Of course I did, sweetheart. Deputy Long brought them in after dark. Is there anything wrong I missed?"

Snow shook his head. "Not if you didn't set a price on them for a customer, dear. These are *rubies,* not garnets."

Longarm blinked and tried to catch Kathleen's eye. He couldn't. So he asked her husband, "Are you sure? And how much money are we talking about?"

Snow shrugged and said, "Oh, say a thousand, fifteen hundred, tops. They're not good quality and they were left baroque because they're too small to cut."

"But they are real rubies, not garnets? The reason I asked is because I sprung mention of mysterious garnets on a suspect earlier today and she's either one swell actress or she didn't know what I was talking about, like she said."

Snow put the gems down and wrapped them for Longarm, saying, "If you don't want them in our safe, make sure you put them somewhere they can't get lost. They're not worth a professional jewel thief's time, but this is a rough town, and I've seen men beaten and robbed for their boots."

Longarm put the stones away. "Would you go over that jewel thief business for me again? I know *you* ain't one. But you must know more than I do about such matters."

Snow nodded. "Naturally, I don't deal in stolen jewels," he said. "But, alas, some do, and word gets around in the trade. Stolen jewelry is fenced for about two-thirds its real market value, since people buying from shady dealers who can't provide too much in the way of papers seldom pay top prices. The fence has to make a tidy profit, and an honest pawnbroker can get his hands on safer merchandise for about a third of its resale value."

Longarm nodded sagely and said, "I follow your drift. A crook would do well getting a fifth of the value and you say one could buy these rocks for no more than fifteen hundred. So whether they was crooked off somebody or not, we're still dealing in three figures, real or not."

It had been a statement, not a question. But Snow was feeling expansive and answered as if Longarm was hard of hearing. Longarm didn't pay much attention, now that he understood what he had in his inside pocket better. He couldn't tell if Kathleen had lied to him on purpose or if the horny little gal had just been showing off more skill than she possessed for anything but screwing. She was managing to look innocent right now. He figured she'd had a lot of practice. He cut Snow's lecture short. "Well, you folks have been more help to me than you'll ever know. So what do I owe you for your time and trouble?" he asked.

Snow smiled graciously and told him to forget it. Longarm shook his head. "Look, the cloth you just saw me stuff away has to be worth something. Your wife spent a lot of time on me before you got here. So I'll tell you what I'm going to do. I'm going to pay for services rendered whether you want me to or not."

He took out two silver dollars and placed them side by side on the glass. As he turned to leave, Snow said, "That's a lot of money for the little we've done for you, isn't it?"

Kathleen at least had the grace to blush beet red and leave the room as Longarm answered soberly, "Nope. I figure I just paid the going rate for what I got here."

Actually, he felt he'd been cheated, when he recalled how they'd been interrupted. But there was no point in symbolism if you failed to do it right. He felt sure Kathleen had got the message, and he hadn't wanted her poor husband to. He strode up to the noisier but safer saloon Doris ran and when he caught her eye she came back to the kitchen to join him. He handed her the wrapped-up rubies and told her, "If you got a safe, I'd like you to keep this for me in it. If you don't, hide 'em good somewhere else."

She took the package but, being a woman, had to ask what was inside. He said, "Evidence. Go ahead and look if you have to. Then make sure nobody else sees 'em till I get back."

She asked when he was coming back as she placed the wad of cloth on a butcher's block to unwrap. Then she forgot all about her own question as she gasped. "Oh, they're so *beautiful!* Are they real, Custis?"

"Yeah. Them's the garnets I told you about. Only they're really rubies, sort of," he told her.

She held them up as if to put them on, but didn't as she sighed. "Gosh they're nice. I'll bet they once belonged to a Hindu princess or something, right?"

"Hindu, Russian, maybe Chinese. They ain't worth

as much as they look like, but they're still worth something. Two gents just tried to gun me to get 'em back. So for God's sake don't let nobody know you got 'em. I hope to come to you by midnight though hell should bar the way. If I don't, you'll know I'm someplace else."

"Oh, have you met other girls in town already?"

He patted her sweet rump and told her, "None I'd trust with my only string of rubies in this world, pard. I ain't being mysterious about my comings and goings, Doris. I just don't know where I might wind up after I leave here. I got a whole mess of loose ends to investigate and up to now I can't even find the damned old knot!"

She kissed him quick and he left, wondering if he'd done the right thing. He liked Doris, and he didn't want to risk her sweet hide on his account. But if anyone knew they were pals they'd likely suspect she was holding the rubies for him in any case and, what the hell, if she had them there was an outside chance she could bargain her life for the fool things. The other way worked out even worse.

He headed down to the docks to see how easy it might be to hire a boat, if he ever needed one. He doubted a local fisherman would carry him all the way to Seattle even if the infernal navy would let him go. But this wasn't horse country, and he sure was getting tired of walking.

He didn't make it to the docks that afternoon. Killer Whale hissed him in between two buildings and said, "You are wanted in Angoon. I think you had better go there, Longarm."

The white man said, "I'll bite; where's Angoon?"

Killer Whale said, "Kootznoowoo."

Longarm said, "Now you *really* got me confused. Try English on me, old son; I understand that a mite better."

The burly Tlingit said, "Katchatag, chief of chiefs,

wants to talk to you. He is very powerful. Every year he gives a big potlatch but even after he's given away everything, even his chilkat, he remains richer than any other real person. He has many coppers, many blankets, more wives than even a young man could ever fuck, and no matter how he tries to give it all away he always has more to give. He is a very important man. Raven smiles on him."

"Yeah, yeah, yeah," Longarm cut in. "I savvy he's a heap big Indian. I already heard about Katchatag from Western Union, so I can make an educated guess about the copper the gods rain down on him. You say this powwow's supposed to take place in the land of hootchy-kootchy?"

"Kootznoowoo. The Stronghold of the Bears. Your people call it Admiralty Island. Don't ask me why. I've yet to see an admiral there, but the place is crawling with bears."

Longarm tried to picture his mental map of the Alaska Panhandle. Admiralty Island was only one island over but it was still an island and he was on another. So he said, "I could spare your chief a few minutes if you could tell me what he wants and how we get there."

"I don't know what he wants with you," Killer Whale said. "But if Katchatag sent for me, and I wanted to go on living, I would go. I know they say we are savages, but real people do not hurt visitors who come in peace, only people who do not want to be friendly. *We* don't have to get there because he did not send for *me*. Come, I will take you to the guide who will show you the way to get there."

Longarm followed the Indian out the far side of the slot before he said, "Hold on, now. Ain't we going the wrong way? If my guide's taking me to another island, how come we seem to be going uphill on this one?"

Killer Whale said, "You talk dumb, for a man who says he knows how to travel this world. All the offshore islands are long and thin. Why go around when one can walk across? Besides, the boat that waits for you on the far shore does not have one of those silly numbers the navy insists we paint on even a seagoing dugout."

"Does the navy even know this mysterious Indian crew has landed in their neighborhood?"

Killer Whale laughed like a barking seal and said, "You are beginning to understand my people. Hear me, Chief Katchatag never signed the peace with the Russians, so why should he sign anything with the weaker Americans?"

"You call Uncle Sam *weak,* pard? Remind me to introduce you to a heap big chief called Sitting Bull one of these days. You could be confusing gentle manners with weakness, and some of your cousins to the south ain't so sure Uncle Sam's even gentle."

Killer Whale shrugged. "Katchatag does not care if your uncle is kind or weak, as long as he stays well away from him. When you meet Katchatag, listen to him before you speak. He is very wise. His words are always good. His temper is terrible."

They were away from town into second growth, now. The husky Indian stopped in a clearing and whistled like a bird. Another bird called back and then a little Tlingit gal wrapped in a chilkat stepped out of the trees to stare at them as if she were looking for a job with a cigar store. Her cloak-like garment was covered with a sort of flattened-out totem pole design in red and black on the light tan of interwoven cedar bark and wool. Killer Whale said, "This is Not Katzeek."

106

"If she ain't Katzeek, who might she be?" Longarm asked.

The girl laughed, tossing her long braids, and said, "Stupid. Not is my *name*. So when I say I am Not Katzeek it means I *am* katzeek."

"Can I just call you Zeke, then?"

"If you like. Come, we must get over the spine of this island before dark."

She turned and walked off into the trees without looking back. Killer Whale muttered, "Follow her. Do not screw her unless she wants you to. She is not one of our mission girls."

Longarm had already figured that out. He said no more to Killer Whale and chased the girl into the trees, glancing up at the sky. The sun was hidden by the low cloud ceiling. He knew it stayed light up here most of the night in summer. So when he caught up with the stocky little gal he asked her what the hurry was, adding, "It's early in the evening. What's the hurry? How wide could this skinny island be, Zeke?"

"About twenty of your miles, half of it uphill and all of it rugged. If we don't reach the other side by the time the bears are feeding along the far shore, the dugout will not be waiting and we will have to wait, in the dark, as the bears decided whether to let us live or not."

He dug out his watch and gave it a more serious look than usual. Then he said, "Zeke, there's no way in hell we're going to hike twenty miles before ten or eleven."

"Not if you walk *that* slow," she said, and leaped lightly up on a rock to show him what she had on under her chilkat, which was nothing. She sure curved in and out mighty nicely for a gal who looked mostly muscle rippling under a smooth copper hide.

He lost interest, even though she had to bend over a lot ahead of him as they struggled up a slope that was just ridiculous to be climbing without a rope. They were beyond the old clear cuts now, and the steep slope between the cathedral-pillar spruce all around wad covered with a treacherous diswelcome mat of silvery dry needles atop pure black slippery muck. He was panting like a steam engine by the time they made it to a level stretch and Zeke said, "Wait. I have to listen before we go on. We could save much time by pushing through those service berries, but sometimes it is wiser to go around."

He drew his .44 thoughtfully and asked, "What are we hunting for, Zeke?"

"It is more important to know what might be hunting us," she said. "Meat is hard to come by in these hills this time of the year. Put that silly gun away. Do you want to get us killed?"

He holstered his .44, but observed, "Generally, when I slap leather, it's the other way around. Are we talking bear, Zeke?"

"Of course. Cougars never attack when it's light. Come, I think it is safe to push on through the service brush."

He didn't know how she managed, as he followed her, getting his legs whipped painfully even wearing boots and pants. The Tlingit girl had on bitty soft deerskin boots like the so-called Apache wore. But her brown legs were bare and, so far, didn't seem to be bleeding. She sure was a tough-skinned little thing. It was odd how legs so hard and tough could look so pretty.

Zeke stopped so suddenly he almost ran over her. She'd stopped breathing as she stared intently at what looked to him like no more than a shoulder-high wall of sticker bush. Then the bear rose up to look back at them.

Longarm stopped breathing, too. He'd seen bear in his time, but this big buffalo-brown bastard made a grizzly look like a cub.

As it stared soberly down at them Zeke started talking to it, softly and politely, in her own lingo as she backed into Longarm. She whispered in English, "Start backing out. Don't run. Don't turn away. For God's sake, don't trip and fall down!"

Longarm proceeded to do so, drawing his gun despite her earlier dismissal of his next-to-useless weapon. Anyone could see stopping a critter that size with a .44-40 slug was as likely as stopping a charging bull with a .22. But if push came to shove he could likely give the bitty gal time to duck out of the way.

He didn't get to find out if he could stop an Alaska bear with a pistol. The bear dropped out of sight in the brush and Zeke said, casually as hell, considering, "Don't run. He's thinking about it. Don't make any moves that might help him make up his mind."

The only moves Longarm and the girl made were backward until at last they were out of the berry patch. "I think we are safe now. I am sorry. That was very foolish of me," Zeke said.

Longarm couldn't argue with that. He asked, "What the hell *was* that critter? When you said bear I thought you meant *bear*, not a house in a fur coat!"

She shrugged. "It was just an ordinary bear. Are the bears smaller where you come from?"

"Sort of," he replied, not ready to holster his gun yet as, off in the brush, he heard something chewing service berries, bush and all.

"Come, we have a longer way to go now," the Indian girl said. "I don't see how we are going to make the far shore before dark, but we have to try. The bear searching for fish along the shoreline are the really dumb ones. So naturally they are more dangerous."

As he followed her—uphill, damn it— he asked her how come bears were likely to be fishing at this time of year, since even he knew it wasn't the fishing season.

"Bears are not as smart as we are," Zeke said. "They don't have to be. When they have found food to eat they go back for more when they get hungry again. This is a hungry time of the year for bears. All the baby beasts are big enough now to run away. Some bears, like the one we just met, are content with berries and grubs. The ones hunting in vain along the shorelines at this time of the year want meat. Any kind of meat, from an ant to an elk."

"You sure talk cheerful in dark woods, Zeke. But what difference do it make whether we meet up with shore bears by day or night? The one I just saw looked dangerous enough by broad day."

The Indian girl looked puzzled. "I thought you said you had bear where you came from," she remarked. "Do you think we'd be alive right now if we'd met that last bear in the *dark?*"

"Oh. Harder to get out of the way, when he can see you and you can't see him, right?"

"Of course. Even bears know this, and I told you they were stupid. They are lazy, too. They don't like to run if they don't have to. So in daylight they are less likely to chase anything. They know, and even the deer know, that meeting a bear in the dark can be safe as getting struck by lightning. It's all over before even a deer could get out of the way."

"Remind me not to meet bears in the dark, then."

"I just did. Don't talk, walk. We have a long way to

go, and the boat crew won't wait if darkness falls before we get there."

Longarm was willing and his flesh wasn't all that weak. But then they ran into a patch of windblow, and even the Tlingit gal had a time getting through such a mess. Trees big enough to build small towns on lay like jackstraws in a mile-wide tangle. Worse yet, it had been some time since a freak squall had knocked them all down at once, and wood rotted fast in this climate. As Longarm ducked under a waist-high timber doorway Zeke had vaulted over the Indian girl turned a horror-struck face to him and gasped, "Are you crazy? You *never* crawl *under* deadwood! If a log breaks under you, you may not get hurt. If it breaks on top of you, you may die fast or you may die slow. But you'll never get a full-grown spruce *off*, once it has you pinned."

He saw what she meant a few minutes later when he followed her over a fallen forest giant that held her soft boot well enough, but gave under his harder heel and left him sitting in a big pile of rotted wood with a dumb expression on his face and yard-long splinters pointed his way from both sides. She reached down to help him up with surprising strength, and muttered, "By Raven's tail feathers, I see now why your kind is always getting lost in our woods."

It got better for a spell on the far side of the windblow. Then it got worse as they came to a ridge of shark-tooth boulders covered with moss and kept wet by the sea breezes sweeping across the high ground day and night. It was getting more like night by the minute as they clambered over the rocks through the mist. He fumbled out his watch, which told a man more than the sun did around here, and said, "It's going on ten-thirty, Zeke.

111

How much daylight do we have left?"

She sighed. "No enough. I know of a cave ahead we can get to before dark, if we hurry."

So they did, and it looked more like a rock shelter than a cave to Longarm. But as darkness fell they built a fire between themselves and the dank dark closing in. Alaska seemed to do every damned thing dramatically. The summer nights were short, but made up for it by being dark as hell, thanks to the constant overcast.

Zeke sat with her back to the mossy wall of the just-big-enough-semi-cavern. As Longarm tossed another damp hunk of deadwood on the fire he could see under her chilkat. He moved into a more pure position and lit a cheroot as he asked her casually how she kept from freezing in the wintertime up here.

She told him Tlingit wore more duds when it snowed, of course, and added, "I don't understand that Jesus business they teach at the mission. I went to the mission school a few summers to learn your language. They made us pray in yet another, but I didn't bother to remember it. The bearded ones spoke foolishly enough when one could understand them. They told us about a first man and a first woman who discovered they could see one another's bodies and had to cover them with leaves. When I asked the bearded one why they were ashamed to see one another naked after they had already fucked, he hit me. Why do you suppose he did that?"

Longarm took a drag and handed the smoke to her as he shrugged and said, "I reckon the idea is that if folk don't see one another naked, much, they'll have more time to praise the Lord and pay taxes. You Tlingit gals don't worry as much about fig leaves, huh?"

"This is good tobacco," she said. Why should women worry about what they have between their legs? Have

112

you ever met a woman who had something *else* down there?"

He chuckled. "Not hardly. But don't it bother your menfolk?"

"Why should it? They know all women are very similar there. It is the other parts that make a woman pretty or ugly, no?"

He said, "Well, I read some place that Arabs think it's pure shocking to see a she-male's naked face. I reckon it's what you was raised to feel shocking as shocks you most. Is that how come you run off from the mission school? You didn't like to wear underdrawers?"

She shrugged. "I did not mind the clothes they made us wear. I don't feel one way or the other about clothes, as long as I am comfortable. I did not run away, either. My people sent me there to learn the new language of the new white eyes. When I had, there was no reason for me to stay longer. It only takes a little while to learn the important things about you people. After that it is just the same old story, over and over. I do not understand why they tell you people the same story every Sunday. Don't they think you can remember a story, even a stupid one, after you've heard it a dozen times or so?"

"I've noticed in my line of work that some nominal Christians do seem to find it hard to recall all the rules. If you mean to get on with white folk, present company aside, don't tell 'em you find the Good Book stupid."

She passed him the cheroot, saying, "I can't help it if the bearded ones have it all wrong. Hear me, they say their big ghost made the world and that he started by making light. That sounds dumb. What sense would there be in building a fire if there was no place to put it?"

"I think the Lord started with the sun and the moon and such, not a campfire, Zeke."

113

She shook her head stubbornly. "That is not the way it happened. In the beginning there was only darkness and Raven didn't like to fly around in the dark like a bat. So he went to the place where Wizard lived and said, 'Hear me, Wizard. I know you have the sun and the moon and the stars in a bentwood box and it is too dark out here. If you give me the sun and the moon and the stars I will give you many coppers.' But of course Wizard said no. He was very old and very selfish. Everyone hates people who are selfish. So Raven hated him, too. He gave Wizard nothing, nothing for the sun the moon and the stars. He stole them while Wizard was drunk and gave them to us and the other animals as potlatch. For Raven is generous, as all good things are."

Longarm resisted the impulse to ask her where Raven, the Wizard, and such might have come from. Theology wasn't his favorite topic even when he wasn't having a conversation with a pretty, almost bare little gal. He took a drag, let it out, and said, "Well, if you ever told that tale to Brother Boris it's a wonder you survived. Getting down to brass tacks, as long as we're discussing Tlingit notions, I got a question perhaps you can answer, Zeke. In town I heard that your folk took it mighty serious when a white man trifled with one of you gals. Yet I know for a fact there's at least one bitty Tlingit in town who sells her all for a nickel. Could you straighten me out on just what the rules might be?"

"It's my turn to smoke," Zeke said. "Our ways are not complicated. If a Tlingit woman likes a man and says she does not mind if he screws her it is nobody's else's business. If a man *forces* himself on a woman he is *wicked*. So naturally the woman's clan, or her owner, has to do something bad to him. It's very simple. I don't know why they made it all so complicated at the mission school."

"Never mind the Christian complications. Back up and tell me what you mean by a woman's owner. You mean her husband?"

She shook her head and said, "We don't go through that business with sad music and everybody getting drunk. If a woman is free she can live with any man she wants to, as long as they are not from the same clan, of course. Most women only live with one man. It seems more natural."

"That sounds mighty free. You say some gals ain't free?"

"Silly, *slaves* are never free. Slave girls can't screw a man even if they like him, unless their master says it's all right. You should never flirt with a Tlingit slave girl. It can cause a lot of trouble."

"I suspicion it already has. I didn't know you folk held with the peculiar institution, Zeke. I doubt if many other white men know it, either. It's no wonder we confuse one another. How does a Tlingit get to be a slave in the first place?"

She shrugged. "Usually by being born a Haida or some other lesser breed. Sometimes, when there hasn't been a war for a long time, Tlingits sell themselves into slavery."

"Sell *themselves?* Don't you mean they get sold by their *parents?*"

"Of course not. That would be a very wicked thing to do. You can sell a captive from another tribe or you can sell your own body, as that belongs to you by natural right. To sell another Tlingit you would have to make war on them. That would lead to all sorts of confusion."

He nodded and said, "You're right. It's confusing as hell. What point would there be in selling your own self into slavery? What would you get out out of the deal?"

"Oh, food and shelter, as well as protection and kind treatment if you chose your master well. Only poor or weak people sell themselves, of course. Sometimes, after a big potlatch, after one has given away everything he owns, a man who has not as many friends as he thought must sell himself into slavery or starve. How do you people manage, if you give away everything you own and nobody gives you anything at all to eat?"

He smiled thinly. "White folk don't hardly ever do that, Zeke."

"How do you prove you are a good-hearted person if you never give everything you own to your friends?" she asked earnestly.

He said, "Our friends don't expect us to be quite that generous, if they know what's good for 'em. But now that I study on it, I can see how your potlatch customs may not be as crazy as some think. Let's see if I got it right. When a Tlingit wants to prove how popular he is, he gives a bit party and passes out all the furniture to the guests assembled, right?"

She nodded. "His cedar boxes, his blankets, his food, even the clothes off his back, if he's really a powerful person."

"What about you gals? Do you sort of give bridal showers and sort of overdo it?"

She shook her head and said, *"Men* give potlatch. *We* are often the *gifts*. Of course a woman given to a friend must be treated well and usually she is given back at the next potlatch."

"I get it. It ain't as dumb as it sounds. It's more like a vote of confidence or a test of power. You give a big party, give everything you own away, then you just have to last some damn way till it's someone else's turn. Then they have to load you down with blankets and such till you're right back where you started?"

"Yes. Only bad people are hurt by potlatch. I don't know why the men with gold stripes on their sleeves say the customs of my people are wicked. Do you?"

"They likely don't understand 'em as well as you do. That's fair. I've had a chore explaining sensible white notions to some Indians in my time, too. When you study on how many whites has killed one another in the name of the Prince of Peace, it's a wonder Indians and whites get along as well as they do."

She looked bored and said, "It won't be dark long. Do you want to fuck?"

He gasped, inhaled wrong, and coughed some before he could manage to reply, "I surely would. But we'd best study on your gracious invite, Zeke. You are taking me to see the big chief of your nation, right?"

"Of course. What's that got to do with whether we like each other or not? You do like me, don't you?"

"Sure I like you, but..."

"Take off your clothes, then. I have never screwed a white eyes and I am curious to see what you look like naked. I don't see how your women know whether they want to screw a man or not. How can they tell, with everyone all covered up all the time?"

He laughed. "Sometimes I suspicion that's why old, ugly white folk invented such proper duds. If Queen Victoria had nicer ankles, skirts would likely be shorter all over."

"Why do you talk so much? Are you trying to say you don't like me? Or do you just like to tease women?"

He laughed again. "I didn't know I was the one with

the teasing ways up here, no offense. You'd be surprised how much I admire you right now, Zeke. But I dunno, a white man walking into an Indian village alone, with a squaw he's trifled with, could wind up feeling nervous as hell."

Zeke pouted and said he was cruel and selfish, adding that the other gals would tease her if she had to admit she'd spent a whole four-hour night with a man who'd never tried to touch her. He asked why she couldn't just brag and she snapped, "What do you take me for, a *liar?*"

So, figuring he was damned if he did and damned if he didn't, he took her in his arms and hauled her in for a friendly kiss. She kissed awful. She pulled her face away from his and asked, "Why did you do that? If feels disgusting. I want you to *fuck* me, not *eat* me."

"Don't you folk kiss?"

"Take off those silly clothes. I'll show you what we do."

He did and she did and it was sort of interesting. As they lay naked together atop her chilkat with the smouldering embers warming their flesh with ruby light, Zeke got on top, impaled herself on his dawning interest, and leaned forward to pant like a dog in his bemused face. He just lay there, enjoying what was going on more natural below their waistlines, until she protested, "Don't you know how to make love, damn it? Open your mouth and pant with me if you really *like* me!"

He tried, trying not to laugh, as they held their open lips almost touching and inhaled one another's breath. She was panting like a steam engine, now, and it was sort of exciting. He might not have liked it as much if she hadn't been screwing him so nice and natural with the parts of her that mattered more. He ejaculated up into her as she panted and sort of whimpered like a happy

118

pup but still kept her kissing distance. He rolled them both over to do it some more, right, and discovered another Tlingit custom that likely took getting used to. She scratched like hell with her nails all up and down his back as he bobbed up and down between her chunky brown thighs.

Her tawny breasts were almost as solid and since he couldn't kiss her lips he settled on a little dark nipple and sucked it hard as he contorted himself into a mighty interesting position. She gasped, "Don't do that. I'm not your mother. *Scratch* my tits if you like them."

He was able to screw better with his back straighter, anyhow. He took the matter in hand and ran a thumbnail back and forth over her turgid nipple as he asked how she like that. She told him to stop fooling around and scratch her hard. She dug her nails deep in his bounding buttocks as she said it, and it hurt. So he tried to see if he could pry her nipple off with his thumbnail and she crooned, "Oh, yes, that feels passionate. I want scratched tits and a bruised back to show the other girls tomorrow. I *knew* you knew how to make love to a woman, once you got over that Jesus nonsense!"

Chapter 9

It was too early to go to work back home, but of course they'd been up for hours by the time they reached the far shore to find what Longarm had assumed would be a canoe waiting for them. The impassive Tlingit crew were sitting in what looked more like a Viking longboat than a canoe, although as he and Zeke got closer he could see it had been carved from one hell of a single tree trunk. The Indians didn't ask where they had been all this time. From the way some of them grinned his way as they paddled off he assumed Zeke must have told them in their own singsong lingo. He understood one or two words that sounded more like the Nadene of the U. S. Southwest. But Tlingit sounded more, "Goo Goo" than the "Hey Nay" way old Cochise had talked the time Longarm had had to sit polite through a long speech.

Once they were out in the channel the Tlingit hoisted a mast and ran up a sail that looked sort of Viking, too, save for being made of bark fibers and painted in a complex design. Tlingit artists had a horror of empty space and odd notions of what faces looked like. But he could make out lots of eyes staring back at him from the sail, so he figured the other stuff had to be teeth, beaks, eyebrows, and such. He looked over the side for a spell to rest his eyes and saw little jellyfish with four-leaf-clover designs on their umbrellas.

He knew nobody ate jellyfish. He asked Zeke what other kinds of sea creatures the bears they had managed to miss along the shore might be looking for. She said there were all sorts of fish, deeper, but that her folk hardly ever ate anything but salmon. She said only poor folk and Aleuts settled for anything less than salmon and he said, "That explains a pure mystery, then. Down in the States, your cousins some call Navaho just won't eat fish, even if they're starving. I always thought it was some religious notion they had. Maybe it is. Maybe, coming down out of the north with tribal memories of what real men ate, they passed up their noses at fresh-water fish until it got to be a habit. Not having salmon in the Southwest desert, they just decided not to eat fish at all and to hell with it."

"Do these Navaho Nadene make potlatch, Custis?"

"No. They used to make the Pueblo give 'em everything, until Kit Carson made 'em stop. Most are sheep herders, now. Their cousins we call Apache ain't decided what they want to do yet. It sure makes it hard to raise horses around 'em."

As Zeke translated the other Tlingit asked questions about their long-lost relatives and seemed to think Apache made piss-poor Nadene until Longarm assured them their distant cousins were considered mean as hell by most.

That cheered them up and they decided the Apache must be Nadene after all.

They sailed on and on until at last they put in to the Tlingit town of Angoon, which looked like a mess of cigar boxes standing on stilts and surrounded by totem poles, with a dark wall of spruce rising behind it. The crew ran the big canoe up on a gravel beach and the resultant crowd almost carried Longarm to a bigger-than-usual stilt house with its door made to look like one was walking into the open mouth of something awful. He lost track of Zeke in the confusion. When his eyes adjusted to the smoky light inside he saw it was an all-stag party. Stone-faced Tlingit sat on benches all around the cedar-plank walls. There was an ornately carved box, chair, or whatever in the middle of the mat-covered floor. An old white-haired man with a plainer-than-usual chilkat over his shoulders pointed at the object and told Longarm to sit on it. So he did. The old man's English was even better than Zeke's as he said, "I am Katchatag. I do not lie. You are Longarm, and I hear good things about you. Do not lie to me and we may be friends. Lie to me and we won't be."

Longarm sat down, nodded soberly, and said, "I don't know enough about you and your people to make up lies about you, Chief. You said you wanted to see me, so here I am."

The old man's eyes twinkled more than he might have wanted them to as he asked, "Did you enjoy the night on the mountain with the guide I sent you, Longarm?"

"I don't lie, either," Longarm said. "But it's against my own customs to talk one way or another about a lady to another man. Did you haul me all the way over here to find out if I liked girls?"

123

Katchatag shook his head soberly. "I was only trying to make you feel comfortable. That is why I sent such a lusty girl to guide you. I know you treat all people with the respect they deserve. You are a good person. You work for the Little Yankee Father. That is a rare combination to find in one man. The blue sleeves in Sitka are fools. I want you to tell the Little Yankee Father this for me."

"Well, to tell the truth, I'm seldom invited to the White House. But I know how stuffy the navy can act. They've been giving *me* a hard time, too. Just what is it you want me to tell my government they've been doing wrong?"

The old man frowned and said, "They do nothing, nothing at all. They treat us as if we were not here!"

"I noticed. But look on the bright side, Chief. Once the B.I.A. gets around to sending regular Indian agents up here to guide your path you might wind up missing the U. S. Navy. I know chiefs down in the States who'd just love to be let alone right now. You're getting paid off regular by Western Union, your gals are free to get paid or not, and even skip school if they don't want to mess with our more civilized customs. So, no offense, I don't see how you're worse off under us than under the Russians."

Katchatag shook his head harder this time. "We had good fights with the Russians. After we taught them it was safer to make slaves of lesser people they left us alone, too. But, better than that, they controlled their own white eyes. When the Russians were here no man could hunt or fish anywhere without a paper from the Little Father and the governor in Sitka did not give the papers to men who might cause trouble. Your navy gives no paper. Like I said, your navy does nothing, nothing. Anyone who wants to can hunt, fish, log, muddy our streams, fuck our women..."

"Hold it right there!" Longarm said with a frown. "Fair is fair, and I know for a fact the navy hangs its own for rape and frowns like hell on anyone else doing it. The town law in Sitka may or may not be as fair. They do have an ordinance forbidding your people from skulking behind saloons and such. So the Tlingit gals peddling their bodies in Sitka are busting white man's law as well as tribal whatevers."

"Do you deny many of our young girls have been abused by white men, Longarm?"

"I can't deny they've been getting laid a lot. Whether it's abuse or not depends on whether they get the agreed price, after, I reckon. Sitka's a tough town. A white man's town. Your folk don't have to go there if they got delicate feelings. Men are men, whether red or white, and when girls come cheap and easy, most men take them as they come. If a white gal came over here and offered to screw one of your young men for some cedar baskets, would you expect us to raise hell about it?"

The old chief laughed, translated, and while some shot daggers at Longarm, more than one chuckled, too. Katchatag said, "They were right about you. You are not a bullshitter. Forget the worthless Tlingit who prefer Jesus and canned food to Raven. White eyes much closer have done worse things. Hear me, everyone knows that unless some salmon get by to spawn, upstream, the river dies. Yet white eyes string their nets across the whole mouth of the river to catch all, *all*, the greedy bastards! How are our grandchildren to eat salmon if selfish strangers put them all in little iron drums for people far away to eat?"

Longarm nodded and said, "They could use hunting and fishing rules and regulations up here, for sure. You'll likely get more than you want in a few years. I'll mention fish hogging to the navy when I go back to Sitka. Don't know if they'll listen or not. Do you have treaty rights to any particular streams?"

Katchatag scowled. "Did they tell you I was a *slave?*" he asked. "Hear me, I have never signed any papers with anybody. The men who make copper wires sing asked me to sign a paper for them so they could give me copper. I told them just to make sure I got copper every summer and nobody would cut their wires. I think they understand me now. Look."

He reached behind him to produce what looked like a totem-pole face hammered flat on a tea-tray-sized slab of burnished copper. He said, "I have many of these coppers, many, but I like this one best. I will hate to give it away the next time I hold potlatch. But Raven hates the selfish. Your loggers are selfish, too. You must have seen what they did to the forest around Sitka. They cut everything, everything, close to the water where it is easy, and leave us only the timber on the high and rocky ground. We do not like to haul timbers to the shoreline any more than they do. They cut without asking if anyone else has prior claim on a tree. You can't carve a good totem pole or fashion a boat from just *any* tree. You have to chose a good one. Sometimes you have to wait a few years until it is just right. How do you think it makes us feel when a total stranger comes along and cuts down a tree we have been waiting for years to cut?"

"It would make *me* sore as hell. Couldn't you post signs on such important landmarks?"

"We do. We are not illiterate. The white eyes who ignore the blazes left on good trees are the ignorant ones. But the ones who give us the most trouble are the ones who seek for yellow copper. They are really crazy, even for white eyes!"

Longarm sighed and said, "I've noticed how some old boys act when they catch gold fever. But do you have enough gold around here for them to bother you for? No offense, but it seems even your copper comes in by Western Union messenger."

The old chief scowled. "There is no gold on Kootznoowoo. We tell them that. They do not listen. They scamper over the inland rocks like goats, breaking off chips with hammers. They shit in our creeks. Worse yet, they muddy them, panning for yellow copper that is not there. You would not believe how much mud a fool can stir up once he's seen mica glittering in it!"

"You're wrong, Chief. I know all about fools and gold. But ain't this whole island your reservation?"

"It is the Stronghold of the Bears. That is my clan. What is a reservation?"

"Never mind. You'll likely find out soon enough, and I want to leave here friendly. I follow your drift and I'll pass on your complaints to some decent gents I know in the B.I.A., whether that'll be doing you a favor or not. I'll warn the navy you folk are mad about trespassers and they'll either send someone to put up 'no trespassing' signs or, it's only fair to warn you, a gunboat. I just can't figure the military mind, either, and I used to have to try."

He had to sit and listen as the old man translated other complaints the other old men wanted to make. When he saw they were running out of steam he raised a hand for silence and said, "I get the picture, and we're starting to repeat it some, Chief. Was there anything else you wanted to ask about?"

Katchatag shrugged. "As long as you are here I may as well pass along the complaints of less important people. I am known for my generosity. Over on the other island the mission Indians I don't consider real Tlingit say a bad woman is stealing a farm some Indians own. They say you know her. She was the one you thought too ugly to breathe with. Why don't you tell her to behave?"

Longarm frowned. "The woman says the farm she's camped at used to belong to her father, Chief."

Katchatag shook his head. "She lies. I knew she had to be evil. The farm belongs to an Indian family. They have not used it for the past few years because someone died there and one must give the spirits time to get used to being dead before one builds a new house nearby. Just the same, it is still their land,and she is digging, digging with a pick and leaving big holes all over the place. Can't you arrest her for that, Longarm?"

Longarm said, "I could if they could prove a white person was exploiting wards of the government, no offense. She says it's her land. Whether she's lying or not, and she likely is, it would take weeks or months even to get the matter into a federal court, which in this case would be naval. I know what she says she's looking for and, between you and me, I want her to find it. At the rate she's going, she likely will, long before we could get an eviction notice to make her stop. Tell your friends she'll go away long before they really need that fallow farm again."

"They are not my friends. They are Christians. What about the ghosts she could be disturbing with all that digging?"

"Hell, they ought to be *Christian* ghosts, when you

study on it. It ain't like *Raven's* likely to take her digging personal, is it?"

The old chief was blessed with his own dry sense of humor. When he translated some of the old gents who had been shooting daggers at Longarm smiled. Katchatag, said, "It is good you believe in Raven. I will say nobody is to hurt the crazy white-eyed woman unless she starts acting as if she meant to stay the winter there. I have other poor relations in Petrograd, you now call it Saint Petersburg. They say a white eyes has been tricking them with wizardry. The other white eyes in Petrograd are bad enough. You are right about an Indian who does not want trouble staying away from such towns. But this one goes out to their villages to play tricks on them. Hear me, if you don't make him stop, some Indian is sure to kill him and I may have to take the war trail again. The bad man's friends are sure to kill the Indian who kills him and my little brothers over there are not strong enough to massacre all the white eyes in Petrograd by themselves."

Longarm gulped and said, "There has to be a better way. Let's see, now, Saint Pete's is . . . Hmm, getting farther from that pending court-martial than I ought to be going. It's on the mainland over a hundred miles from here, ain't it?"

"On the mainland, but less than a hundred miles. We could get you there in one day. Two days back to Sitka, by sea, since there would be no point in going overland from that far south."

"I'm sorry, Chief. That's still cutting it a mite thin. But I can tell the navy and I'm sure they'd rather send a shore patrol after one bad white than the Tlingit Nation. What's his name?"

The old chief consulted with the other tribal elders before he nodded and said, "Smith. I remember now. His first name is funny, too. They call him Soapy, Soapy Smith. He plays mean tricks on Indians with bars of soap. A decent white eyes in Petrograd told one of our people the soap this wizard sells as magic only cost a few cents in the general store in Petrograd. Have you ever heard of such a cheat?"

Longarm nodded soberly. "He was doing much the same to white folk, last time we met. But are you sure it's the same Soapy Smith? Last I heard, reliable, Soapy Smith was said to be up in Skagway, cheating at cards."

Katchatag nodded. "It must be the same person. We were told the other white eyes ran him out of Skagway for some reason. You will tell the navy somebody ought to arrest him before one of our people kills him?"

Longarm rose, saying, "There's no somebody but *me* involved, now that I know who we're talking about. I meant to go after the son of a bitch personal. So let's get cracking!"

Chapter 10

It was late at night with the low, red, sullen sun pretending to be the moon when Soapy Smith began to suspect he'd worn out his welcome in the tough little town of Saint Pete. The tinhorn was seated in a corner of the Dirty Dog dealing dirty poker as he tried to make up his mind whether or not to deal honest just this one time. The sullen-looking bearded gent across the table was starting to get that look in his eye and neither of the other two gents at the table looked too happy about the way the game had been going up until now, either.

Soapy Smith was too professional to be caught dealing crooked. But he'd learned in the past to his considerable disgust that some gents were just poor losers, whether they could figure out how you were doing it to them or not. Soapy Smith was not a sissy. He'd once slapped leather on the famous Longarm—not knowing who it was at the time, it was true, but why spoil a good story—so he figured he could take any of the sullen rascals if he had to. But three to one seemed lousy odds to a slicker who preferred the odds to be in his own favor even when he was only betting money.

He decided, what the hell, he'd built the modest stake he'd bilked some fool Indians out of to a mighty fine night at this table and it made more sense to give some of it back and leave with the rest than to wind up with nothing or all, depending on who drew first.

He dealt from the top this time, not even trying to see what he was dealing, as he met the suspicious glare of the spoilsport across the way with an innocent smile. Soapy Smile was good at looking innocent, even if he wasn't as good-looking as he thought he was. Nobody could have been as handsome, or as smart, as Soapy Smith thought he was.

When they all picked up their hands, Soapy Smith turned sort of green. For, not even trying, he'd dealt himself a full house. He gulped, put the cards face down, and said, "I'm out." That should have ended it. One of the three had to have *some* damned kind of cards, and since he had no claim on the pot right now, why was that bearded wonder still glaring at him so?

Soapy found out when, after a few raises, one of the other suckers said, "Read 'em and weep." and turned over half-ass straight with deuces wild. The bearded brooder spread his useless mix of low cards on the table but stared hard at Soapy Smith instead of his losing hand as he snapped, "God damn your mother's sour milk, you done that on purpose! I seen you deal that bottom deuce to your sidekick, Smith!"

It got very quiet in the Dirty Dog Saloon. The piano

in the far corner died with a whimper and gents who had business elsewhere went to attend to it. As the barkeep took down the mirror Soapy Smith said soberly, "Mr. Hoskins, here, ain't my sidekick, Mr. Bleeker. As he'll tell you himself, I've been beating him pretty good all evening."

Hoskins started to rake in the pot, muttering, "If there's one thing in this world I plead innocent on, it's going partners with Soapy Smith, Bleeker. What's got into you tonight?"

"Shark teeth," Bleeker said. "You think I don't know this oily son of a bitch was run outten Skagway for cheating at cards?"

Soapy Smith said softly, "That's the second time you've mentioned my mother, Mr. Bleeker. Call me a card shark if you like, but let's leave personal remarks out of this business discussion. I'm pained to learn Mr. Hoskins doesn't admire me either, but he's telling you true. I journey through life alone in this wicked world and if I was dealing dirty the last thing I'd deal would be a losing hand to my own self. I just did. So why don't you grow up? You knew who I was when you sat down to play in this sandbox with the rest of us kids, Bleeker."

It might have worked. Bleeker was starting to look doubtful and Hoskins was looking as innocent and out-raged as he no doubt felt. Then the hitherto silent player to Soapy's right said, "Let's see that losing hand you just dealt yourself, Soapy."

The tinhorn looked at him as if he'd just crawled out from under a wet rock and said, "I thought you were a card player, Mr. Wade. Since when does a man who drops out have to show his cards?"

"Since Wade asked you to," said Bleeker flatly, scraping his chair back to give his gun hand elbow room.

Soapy Smith kept smiling, but his eyes went dead as he asked in a deadly purr, "Before I answer that last request, let's see how this deal stacks up, gents. I make it Bleeker and Wade on one side. Where do you stand, Hoskins?"

The winner left his winnings on the table as he slid his chair back. "I'm out, if it's all the same with the other players."

Bleeker stared soberly, nodded grudgingly, and growled, "Leave the pot and git, then. Old Soapy, here, was about to show us why he's so coy about showing cards he says ain't important. Ain't that right, Soapy?"

Soapy Smith didn't answer. He was too busy trying to figure which one would be the fastest. He was in one hell of a mess even if he guessed right.

Hoskins got up from his chair and took off. Longarm stepped into the pool of light over the table and slid the vacated chair closer before he sat down, placed his .44 on the table in front of him, and said, "I'm in. What are the stakes?"

Bleeker's jaw dropped and Wade said, "Hold on, now. You already got your gun out, stranger."

Longarm said, "I know. But what the hell, we wouldn't be having such a tense conversation if everyone agreed this was an *honest* game. Evening, Soapy. How's your gun arm tonight?"

Soapy Smith's face was expressionless but little wheels were spinning in his eyes now as he replied soberly, "Tolerable, Mr. . . . ?"

"I think you for disremembering my name, Soapy. It do make the situation simpler, don't it?"

"To a point. I'm still trying to figure out whether

you're with me or them."

"Hell, Soapy, I never met either of these gents before, and we have had some fun together in the past. So how do you reckon we ought to work this out?"

Soapy Smith leaned back, both hands off the table, and said, "Your deal, pard."

Longarm nodded, smiled at the others, and said, "Here's how I see it, gents. You know Soapy's rep. In all modesty, I'm a faster draw, and my gun's already out. You boys may be good enough to take on two established gunslicks, two against two. But if you was that good *you'd* be famous, too, and you *ain't.*"

Bleeker asked, "Who are you, if you're so good?"

Longarm answered, "If I wanted you to know, I'd tell you. But I don't, so I won't. You boys can just back off easy, with no women watching, or you can...Soapy, cut that out. If I was ready to kill these boys they'd be dead right now, you fool."

"Well, Bleeker said bad things about my mother, damn it."

"I know, Soapy. I heard him. But I'm sure he's sorry and now he's going to get up, with his hands friendly, and just walk on out. Ain't that true, Bleeker? I *hope* it's true, for I get surly as hell when I'm called a liar."

Bleeker slowly rose, hands out to his side, as Hoskins seemed eager to do the same. Bleeker said, "All right. Just let me have my own money back from that pot and I'll forget about it."

Soapy Smith might have been willing, but Longarm shook his head and said, "I was watching the game a spell before I saw fit to sit in. You anted up and you lost. You bullied the winner away from the table and out the door. So under the house rules, when a pot ain't been claimed, it reverts to the house, and my old pal Soapy had the deal when you two started betting bullets instead of money."

Wade asked, "Who says what the house rules are here?"

Longarm said, "I do, unless you aim to change my mind for me the hard way. I wouldn't advise it. That old '74 you're packing too high would be a mighty dumb thing to go for when a man's got the drop on you with a double-action, Mr. Wade."

"Come on, Wade. We got to go study on this unfair situation in private," Bleeker said.

As the two left the now-empty saloon, Soapy Smith let out his breath with a long wheeze. "I never thought *you*, of all people, could turn out to be so fond of me, Longarm. You want half the pot, of course?" he asked.

"Damned A. I earned it. Are we square on that little misunderstanding we had down in Denver, Soapy?"

"We surely are. Does that mean I can come back to Denver?"

"Don't get sickening about it. I don't like you *that* much. To tell it true, I just saved your ass because I need it somewhere else right now. The local Indians are getting set to kill you, too. You really ought to be ashamed of yourself, Soapy."

"I am, but a man's got to eat. Am I under arrest?"

"No. Unfortunately, I can't come up with a federal charge that would stick, and you know it. You're too tinhorn to get on my list of wants. Before I tell you about it, we'd best douse that lamp."

He stood up and trimmed the lamp above the table, plunging their corner in gloom, now that all the light came in from the late-night sky out front. Soapy asked, "You reckon they'll come back with help?"

"We'll have the light behind 'em if they do," Longarm

answered. "It would be smarter for them to wait outside for us. So we'd best wait until dark. Now shut up and let me tell you what you're going to do for me and the U. S. Navy."

He explained about the naval deserter claiming to be Soapy Smith. The tinhorn said, "I've never been so insulted in my life, and you just heard that rascal call me a son of a bitch. You're sure all I have to do is appear in court and swear that other no-good bastard ain't me?"

"Soapy, you know if I was out to arrest you I'd arrest you. I ain't one for fancy tricks when I know for sure I can beat a man to the draw. You ain't wanted federal, so the navy can't arrest you, neither, much as it might want to. So how about it? Do we have a deal?"

Smith held out his hand and they shook on it. Then he put his own gun on the table and started dividing the pot with Longarm as he said, "I may like it better in Sitka. I've never seen such an unfriendly town as this one, and I left Skagway one jump ahead of the vigilance committee."

"What did you do up there, Soapy? Same as tonight?"

"Oh, hell, I was almost *there* in Skagway. I mean to go back as soon as tempers cool. I got a piece of a whorehouse and exclusive deal in a saloon across skid row. I left some money there with a gal who'll always be true to me, if she knows what's good for her. I got to recruit some backing afore I go back, though. You wouldn't be interested in owning half a town, would you, Longarm?"

"I got a job. What's so special about Skagway, Soapy?"

"It's the end of the line. The last port of call for steamers up the Inland Passage. From there on into the interior you got to mush. A gent who controls Skagway will control all the land and water shipping, both ways!"

"Do tell? You must have heard them yarns about gold in the interior, huh? What if there ain't no gold, Soapy?"

"Hell, it don't matter. I'm a businessman, not a ragged-ass prospector. You give me control of the Skagway docks and it won't matter if they find gold over to the Yukon or not. Nobody's going to get to *look,* without paying tribute to yours truly! This here territory figures to be important someday soon, and for once I'll be in on the ground floor!"

Longarm pocketed his own share of the winnings. "Make sure you don't wind up under the ground while you're at it, Soapy. I won't chide you about your career so far, now that we're going to be pards for a few days at least. But you ain't got it in you to be an empire builder. If the town you mean to take over ever gets worth taking over, bigger and meaner men will be arriv-ing to do so."

"Oh, hell, I'm pretty tough. I just showed *them* two, didn't I?"

"Nope. *I* did. It's getting darker, now. Just sit by my side, little darling, and it may be safe to sneak out the back way in a few minutes."

"How can we be sure they ain't covering the back, Longarm?"

Longarm looked disgusted and told the dark ceiling, "Listen to him, will you? He's got so good at cheating Indians he thinks he's a man of conquest." Then he ex-plained, "We just bullied a town bully-boy. He'll either stay bullied, come back the way he went out with friends, or be waiting out front to see if we want a showdown. He thinks he's brave. So he must think we're even braver. Why would a couple of wild Westerners like us go skulk-ing out the back way like yaller dogs, or the experienced travelers we are?"

Smith chuckled. "Travel do broaden one. But by the way, where are we supposed to go once we sneak out? The whole damn town ain't a hoot and a holler across and Bleeker owns a lot of it."

Longarm nodded. "That's why I'm hoping he won't expect us to make a run for it. He knows, or thinks he knows, we got no place to run."

"So where *do* we have to run, Longarm?"

"Indian sailing canoe, down the beach a mile or less. I left it there so I could drift in quiet. I feared you might misread my intent if I approached you more open."

"You figured right. But I ain't sure Indians like me, Longarm."

Longarm laughed. "Why should they? Nobody else does. I told the big chief of the Tlingit not to kill you before me and the navy is done with you. So let's not worry about my Indian crew. Let's worry about *getting* to 'em. It's as dark as it's likely to get up here in summer, now, so let's go."

They did, taking the usual precautions and making it across the back yard and over a fence without getting shot at. The midnight sun had to go down at least a little, this far down the Alaska coast, but as they headed into the spruce along the shore north of town the gray sky was still lighter than a full moon could have managed in other parts. Longarm was looking ahead for the canoe, assuming they'd made it. So he was startled when a familiar voice ran out, "There they are, boys! I told you they'd make for their squaws, the bastards!"

That was the last thing Hiram Bleeker ever said. When Longarm and Soapy Smith saw a dozen club-swinging rascals coming out of the trees at them, they both fired first at the gent directing traffic. After that it was open season. Smith dropped two and Longarm blew away another before the mob reconsidered a move that had been pretty dumb to begin with and crawfished back into heavy cover.

Longarm snapped, "Let's go!" and started running, reloading as he ran, with Smith crunching gravel right behind. They made it around a big bend, spotted the dim form of the dugout, and got to it just as someone in the woods came unstuck and started pegging blind shots through the trees at nothing in particular.

The Tlingit crew had assumed from their manner of arrival that they might be in a hurry. So they were already starting to paddle as Longarm boosted Smith over the side and followed. As they both sat up on the damp cedar bottom Soapy Smith laughed and said, "Hot damn! That'll larn Bleeker to mention a gentleman's mother in a saloon. Are we in trouble with the law in Saint Pete, now? You'd know more about such matters, being a lawman and all."

Longarm sighed. "*I* ain't in trouble. They don't know me there. If you're smart, you won't go back. I can't square town law or town grudges. You sure are starting to get the rep a man might need to take over a town, Soapy."

Smith laughed again. "I know. Thanks, Longarm. I ain't sure I could have took the town bully of Saint Pete on my own. But now I'm sure to get the credit for it. So put her there, pard!"

Chapter 11

Tacking against the wind, even having to paddle some, the seagoing Tlingits got Longarm and his witness back to Sitka before the navy got its admiral back. Longarm introduced Soapy Smith to the gents at the officers' club, warned them not to play cards with him, and took him aside. "Look, Soapy. You can raise all the hell you want here after I'm gone. But until the trial I want you to behave. I mean it."

Smith shrugged and said, "I got the grubstake from Saint Pete to last me a few days, if I don't meet nobody prettier than you. Where are you heading now, Longarm?"

"To see somebody prettier than me, of course. Oh, there's gals in town I want you to stay away from as well. The dishwater blonde in the assay office is easy, but her husband packs a ten-gauge and she's indiscreet as hell. You may hear tell of a mysterious woman digging

141

for diamonds on an old abandoned farm. Don't go help her. You can mess with anything else you run into, and some of it ain't bad. When you find a place to stay, leave word at the first saloon off the post, and don't mess with Doris, either."

"You sure know the she-males in this town, Longarm. I confess I'm starting to feel left out."

"Doris is mine and I'm doing you a favor by telling you to steer clear of the other two. You ain't near as smart as me and they both nearly got me in trouble."

"Which one's the best?"

"The blonde," Longarm lied. "Stay away from her anyhow."

He knew Smith probably would. But if he did tempt fate there was less mystery to what old Kathleen was up to and he didn't want a professional crook like Soapy Smith anywhere near a gal digging for diamonds.

He went to see if Doris still had the rubies. She did. It was nowhere near closing time, but Doris turned the bar over to the old geezer who usually just swamped and dragged Longarm upstairs to show him how much she'd missed him. As they made love in the same old familiar way, Doris said, "I was sort of expecting never to see you again, Custis. I ain't no crybaby, but will you promise me something?"

He asked her what her pleasure might be.

"I want you to promise that when it comes time for you to leave, you'll at least come by to say goodbye and, well, mayhaps do this one last time."

He said he would if he could. She said, "I promise not to act sad. It's just that I've been feeling so up-in-the-nowheres the last few nights, not knowing if you was ever coming back or not. You understand what I mean?"

"Sure, honey. A gal has a right to know."

"There'll no doubt be another you, someday," she went on. "But it won't be you."

Doris slid out from under him, hunkered down to take the rubies she'd hidden in a drawer, and put them on, letting the red stones sparkle between her pretty bare breasts as she stood up. She moved over to the bed again, saying, "I was looking at myself in the mirror last night. Don't I look swell? I know these jewels is evidence and all. But would you mind my wearing 'em some, just up here, private? They make me feel sort of special."

He told her she was special and added, "Keep 'em on all the time if you like. They make you look real high-toned, Doris."

"I don't know why, but having such fancy jewelry on makes me feel like a real high-class gal instead of just a barmaid," Doris said.

He pulled her down, kissed her tenderly, and said, "You was already high-class when I met you, honey. You're a saloon owner, not a barmaid."

"I know, but it's such a bitty little place in such a bitty little town. What do your reckon a set of jewels like this would cost me, if I saved up to send away for 'em, Custis?"

He didn't tell her how much they were worth. It could hurt her either way. He started to remount her. She said, "Wait. I want to get on top this time, queenly."

So he let her, and he had to admit she looked grand as she bobbed up and down above him with the rubies bouncing all over her. He told her so and she said, "I know. I can see us in the mirror when I get on top like this."

Doris sat up straighter with him in her as she stared at herself in the mirror and said, "You know, I do look mighty proper right now, save for being bare-ass naked.

143

I seen pictures of ladies who lived long ago, when folks didn't wear nothing but fig leaves, and they still managed to look proper, even with their tits showing. You ever seen them sort of pictures, Custis? I don't mean the dirty Frenchy ones. I mean them high-toned goddess gals."

He assured her he knew what she was talking about and that she was a worthy rival to your average Greek or Roman goddess.

Doris raised her arms to clasp her hands behind her head. It did wonders for her bustline, rubies and all. He said, "Uh, could you move a mite faster if you want to stay up there, honey?"

She replied by gripping down tighter with her velvety insides as she moved up and down, straight-backed as a lady posting on a thoroughbred. She gave a little giggle. "I think I'm fixing to come. You can't tell, in the mirror. If someone was spying on us I'd look ever so proper.

"I'm moving. I'm moving. I'm...oh, yesss, I'm coming!"

He rolled her on her back to finish right and she came again because of the way she'd been teasing them both. He didn't notice she was crying until he'd satisfied himself. When he did, he kissed her and asked what was the matter now.

"I'm sorry. I didn't mean to put on airs. I knows what I am. It's just that, well, Custis, I wish I *was* a high-toned woman."

He didn't know how to make her feel more dignified without treating her less dignified. So he just kissed her, groped for his shirt, and fished out a cheroot. He lit up, snuggled her head against his chest, and offered her a drag. She said, "Wait," and took off the rubies before she snuggled closer and said, "Now I can smoke cigars again."

He didn't ask why. He could see how a high-toned gal wearing jewelry would look sort of odd puffing on a three-for-a-nickel smoke.

She helped him kill the cheroot, stretched like a kitten, and said, "If I don't get back up, I'm going to fall asleep, and I can't trust Pop ahint the bar too long at a time. You go ahead and sleep if you like, darling. You're going to need your strength when I close for the night and come back up."

He told her he had chores, too, so they both got dressed and parted friendly. She didn't even ask him where he was going, bless her good nature. He sure wished there was something a man like him could do for a gal like her, but there wasn't. So he headed on out to see if he could do anything for Tasha.

He heard her busting gravel with her pick before he came out of the trees. Her hair was down and her shirt was sweaty, so he didn't ask if she'd had any luck. Nobody was about to work this hard after what should have been sundown once they found what they were digging for.

Tasha stood up in the latest hole she'd dug, bracing her no-doubt aching back with one hand as she rested the other on the pick handle. She wheezed, "I never expected all these rocks. I don't see how they ever farmed here. The soil's half gravel and the other half is bigger stuff."

He lit a smoke before he suggested, "I'd look for a patch where the rocks is stuck in different. I can see from here you're digging in never-dug glacial till, Tasha. That ain't what I come out here to talk about, though."

She glanced up at him, batty-lashed, to ask, "Oh, and what *did* you come for? I don't see why you'd want to go to strangers, and I have to admit I'm feeling even naughtier, tonight. Why don't we go inside?"

"I just come out from inside. I got information to trade with you, Princess. It don't matter whether you've told me the entire tale or not. Whether you're working a lawful claim or just digging for the treasure on other folks' land, the Indians have been watching you."

She looked around sort of wild-eyed, and he said, "You can't see 'em. With Indians it generally works the other way. They asked me to run you off. Leave your damned buttons alone. I said it made more sense just to let you dig up your whatever and leave peaceable. So they ain't fixing to attack your cabin just yet. But you are running low on time. I got a witness for that court-martial and as soon as it's done I'll be leaving for Seattle. If you know what's good for you, you'll be catching the same boat. Once I'm gone, I can't protect you no more, and if you tell the navy what you're doing here they might ask all sorts of fool questions. Especially if this ain't really your old homestead."

She sighed and said, "A girl just can't keep any secrets from you, can she?"

He nodded, not showing his cards until he knew what game she was playing this time. "All right, so old Rostov was my lover, not my father, and I'm really French Canadian," she admitted.

"I figured you had to be sort of French."

"Don't be nasty. You know you liked it. Seattle sent you my prison record, right?"

"Something like that."

She shrugged fatalistically. "All right, so I stole some jewelry when I was working as a French maid for a mean old bitch who didn't pay her help. What of it? I did my time and her damned old jewels were insured, anyway."

He blew a thoughtful smoke ring and didn't answer,

for he'd seldom met a thief who didn't try to justify his or herself with the same old Robin Hood story. On the other hand, once you got them telling how noble they were, deep down inside, there was no telling what else they might let slip. He took a stab in the dark by saying, "Seattle says they ain't sure you gave your right name when you was arrested that time."

It worked. "I'm really Yvette Blanchard. It was my first arrest and I didn't know the ropes. Old Rostov let me use his name even though we never married officially. He did have a daughter named Natasha, and he did leave the diamonds up here, as I said."

"Only he was scared to come back for them because *our* law, not the Russian law, was likely keeping an eye on him?"

She sighed. "Yeah, there's no sense trying to hide it, now that he's dead, and he did die of natural causes, in case you've been avoiding me because of that suspicion. Seattle must have told you he fenced everything from furs to railroad locomotives. But he said he'd never had his hands on such grand diamonds since he had to leave them behind up here. So here I am, and what happens now?"

Longarm thought for a moment. "There ain't much the law can do about it if you dig 'em up, you slick little critter. By rights you really ought to stake a mining claim, I reckon. But that ain't my department and, so far, the navy's been letting everybody save Indians gut and get. I want you to study my words before you answer my next question, Tasha, if I can still call you that."

"I wish you would. It's the name on my return passage, and they treat a Russian princess ever so much nicer than a French maid."

"So be it; Tasha it is. I've told you true, more than

once, you are welcome to any jewels you dig up here in Alaska. I still can't figure out why you or some damned somebody put a string of garnets, rubies, or whatever in my infernal pocket. I said garnets the last time because that's what a fibbing or foolish gal told me they was. Does it make any more sense to you as rubies?"

She just looked blank. He said, "Damn it, Tasha. I told you you could have 'em *back,* if they're *yours!* I can't arrest you for stuffing 'em in my pocket. Giving presents ain't a federal crime. It ain't a valuable enough string to be seriously hot. So do you want it back or don't you?"

She laughed and said, "If the jewelry's not valuable, what on earth would I do with it? Seattle must have told you I only stole good stuff in my wild younger days. You can throw your garnets or whatever away, for all I care. Why all this fuss over a string of cheap stones?"

He said, "Somebody wanted 'em enough to send a pair of hired guns after me. One mentioned 'em in passing as he passed away. I hate to admit this, Tasha, but if you wanted them play-pretties enough to kill for 'em, you'd never have stuffed 'em in my pocket and you wouldn't be refusing 'em now."

She shrugged. "Oh, hell, I'll *take* them, if you're giving them away *free.* I won't accept them as payment, though. I told you I was a warm-natured woman, not a whore."

He smiled and said he had to allow that. "I can't give 'em to anyone but someone claiming 'em as their rightful owner just yet. But I'll keep you in mind," he told her.

She arched an eyebrow. "Pretty slick, but no thanks. I tell you, I never saw the stones you're talking about. So I'm not about to claim them as mine, you sneak. Why don't we sneak inside and get sneaky in a nicer way?"

He might have. Hell, he *would* have, under other circumstances. But he sighed gallantly and said, "I can't take you up on your kind offer just yet, either, no offense."

"Maybe on the boat going back to the States, Custis?"

He just grinned knowingly and she winked and got back to work. She sure could swing a pick hard. He wondered if they'd had her on the rock pile in that women's prison.

He went back to town to see what Portland, not Seattle, had wired back. They'd wired next to nothing, since they'd never heard of any furrier called Rostov. He chuckled. Old Tasha had slipped up, passing that remark about Seattle after assuring him all wide-eyed and innocent she was a poor little orphan from Portland. He wired the Seattle police just in case she'd tried to flimflam him again. He doubted it, unless she was even smarter than he was. She sure had a mess of wheels going around inside of other ones inside her pretty little head.

He heard the gunshots as he came out of the Western Union office. It sounded like both barrels of a ten-gauge. The Snows' shop was down that way, so Longarm joined the crowd as others popped out to have a look-see.

He saw he was right when he got to the assay office and found the town law and a deputy in the busted-open doorway. The town law hissed, "Get under the jamb with us, Longarm. He's upstairs, with a ten-gauge in his hands and murder on his mind."

Longarm got quickly under the overhang, drawing his own gun as he asked, "Who are we talking about? Has the Snows been held up?"

The town law shook his head. "Only one of 'em. The wife's in the back, dead, under a dead sailor boy. Snow come home unexpected and blew 'em both away. At least, that's the way she reads. I can't get anyone around here to talk to me about what happened. The wife and her lover can't and Snow won't. But he can't get away and he has to get hungry. I got boys out back and all the food and water in town if he means to make a siege out of this."

Longarm moved back through the shop. That air still reeked of gunsmoke until he got to the back room where he had almost been caught with Kathleen. There was blood spattered all over the wallpaper above the bunk. The sailor had been a nice-looking kid.

Longarm went to the back steps and put a boot up a couple of risers as the town law came back to tell him he was crazy. Longarm said, "I ain't *that* crazy. I might be able to talk him down."

"What the hell for? He can't get away."

"Don't you ever want folk to use the main drag no more? He's got it covered from his front windows, you know."

"Oh, go ahead, but watch yourself, son."

Longarm did. He called out, "Mr. Snow? It's me, Deputy Long. I was in here the other day about rubies, remember? I want to talk to you some more. I just figured something out."

There was a long silence. Then a sad, lost voice called down, "Go away, Deputy. I'm not going to hurt anyone else if I don't have to. But I've reloaded and I swear I'll blast you."

"Now why in thunder would you want to do that, Snow? You know as well as me you'll get off on the unwritten law, if you don't hurt nobody else."

"I've just murdered my wife, you idiot! As soon as I can get up the nerve I mean to take my own life. But I can't find any liquor up here! That bitch must have given it to her boy friend!"

Longarm kept his voice deliberately calm as he called back, "I know it's wrong to speak ill of the idea, but she bitched me, too. Crack the door wider and I'll tell you how."

"I can hear you. What do you mean, Kathleen bitched you? Don't tell me *you* were one of her lovers, too!"

Snow had asked him not to, so Longarm didn't. "She bitched me more serious. She tried to flimflam me and get me killed. Do you remember them rubies I left in your safe, the ones she assayed for me as garnets worth a heap less?"

"Look, I don't want to discuss cheap jewelry right now. I just killed two people and I think I'm about to throw up."

"Hell, they can't look as bad from up there as they do from down here, Snow. You ought to feel sorry for that sailor boy, though. He was as much a victim as you and me."

"What could that man I just caught making love to my wife have to do with your confounded rubies, Deputy?"

"Nothing. She was just screwing him for practice. She was out to screw you and me in a more practical way. But when it didn't work she just went back to being wayward. Come on down and I'll tell you all about it."

Snow's voice was curious but still desperate as he called down, "I can hear you well enough from up here. How could any woman screw her own husband worse than I just caught her doing it?"

"She was planning all along to leave you, first decent chance she got. Don't ask me about that part. You'd know better than me why. I come in as a golden opportunity while you were out of town. I had a string of not-too-valuable, but still-worth-something rubies. You told me they was good for maybe fifteen hundred dollars, or near three years' wages for the sort of gent she'd have run off with if she could find him. She didn't think she could run off with me, but she could see I didn't know what the rocks was worth. She told me they were worth less. So like a chump I even asked her to hang on to them for me. That's when she got an even better notion than offering me less than they was worth. She had lots of old boys fond of her, as you might have just noticed. One was a nice-enough-looking hired gun called Tex Jones. He wasn't willing to run off with her. But when she told him about the jewels they could both see that if I never came back to claim 'em, she'd be ahead by a string of rubies. Not fair with any man, save in bed, she likely told her dangerous boy friend they was only garnets, but that she'd split the five hundred or so they were worth with him if he'd make sure I never reclaimed 'em. He recruited another rat who'd have gunned his grandmother for a double eagle and together they lay in wait for me just down the block, figuring to gun me the next time I got near this shop. I made it even easier by walking in on 'em. Only they weren't as good as they thought. Then, as you'll recall, I did come back, you did get the gems out, and you naturally appraised 'em closer to their true value."

"My God, I was wondering why Kathleen acted so nervous around you, Deputy! I think I owe you an apology. I knew she was fooling around with somebody. But if you killed her real lover..."

"I said she had no choice but to forget the notion for now," Longarm continued. "Since I didn't act suspicious of her, fool that I am, and the only men who knew what she'd planned was dead, she just acted cool as a sweating cucumber and decided she might have better luck another time. Don't tell me if you told her you were going away on business again and come back unexpected. I can guess good, but if you say it, we'll have you on premeditated. As it now stands, there ain't a jury in the world as wouldn't let you off for acting natural down here just now. So toss down the shotgun and let's see about a lawyer for you, hear?"

There was a long silence before Snow replied dully, "I knew what she was. I kept trying to tell myself I was just a suspicious fool. But I was only fooling myself. You remember that day you had the gunfight with her lover? I'm sure I almost caught her that time."

"I'm just as glad you didn't. Come on, pard; she wasn't worth it, and we both know it."

Snow sobbed, "I know what she was. I know she wasn't worth it. I know most sensible men would have left her long ago. But, God help me, I loved her, and I just don't see how I can live without her!"

Longarm didn't mention the obvious option. But old Snow must have figured it out for himself. Longarm stiffened as he heard both big shotgun barrels go off at once. Then, before the poor fool could reload, he was up the stairs and through the door.

He lowered his own gun and muttered, "Aw, Snow, why did you have to go and do a fool thing like that?" as he stared down at the mangled corpse at his feet.

Chapter 12

Doris wasn't serving much trade that evening and the one whore holding up the piano looked sort of lost with nobody playing the piano. Doris said it was because the fishing fleet was out late for some reason, and that it was just as well, for she was even more short-handed right now. She asked Longarm if he'd seen Pop in his recent travels. Her swamper was one of those little gray cats nobody every looked at, so Longarm couldn't say for sure.

Doris held a beer schooner up to the light, sighed, and said, "Oh, well, who's likely to notice, once this is full of beer? I got to really clean my glassware sooner or later, though. Pop's so blind he wouldn't notice a lump of coal stuck to glass, and he will leave soap scum. Maybe if I can manage to close early I can give all this glass a good hot rinse. I keep telling him and telling him you're supposed to rinse the old soap *off*, not put more *on*. But good help is hard to find these days."

Longarm said, "I'll give you a hand if you mean to do the dishes this side of early in the morning. How come you can't get enough help. There's mission Indians down the shore hungry enough to raid garbage cans. Surely a sharp-eyed young Tlingit could rinse out glasses better than an old half-blind white drunk."

Doris nodded but said, "Already thought of that. Can't do it. Town ordinance won't let them work in this end of town. I don't mind telling you it makes me mad as hell. I've had to turn away squaws begging for a job at my back door, and then come out here myself to keep house late at night after hours."

"How come? Is it because you're so close to the naval base? I know the Tlingit used to be Russian subjects, but I'm sure the Tsar would send white spies, if he was at all interested.

Doris shook her head. "I asked the navy. They said they don't care where Indians go, as along as it ain't their officers' club. They even have some Tlingit dock workers on the base. They give 'em special passes to get through this end of town as well as their gate. I asked the town council why I couldn't have a couple of Indian kids to do chores no white around here will hire out for and they said they was afraid I'd wind up screwing them. That ain't the way they put it. But I knew what they meant and asked 'em how often they'd heard of a squaw raping a white woman. They got all red-faced and said there was no telling *what* a savage might do."

Longarm looked disgusted and growled, "If there's one way to make anyone savage, treating 'em savage is it. They ain't worried about morals or you wouldn't have so many whores in here when the fleet's in. Keeping the mission Indians away from the jobs they could likely get in town means work and wages for whites who might not otherwise be worth hiring. Would you fire Pop if I could get you some Indian help, pard?"

Doris shook her head and said, "That would be mean. He swamps all right and he needs the job. I could even let him spell me ahint this bar if his hands were more free and I didn't leave him unsupervised too long at a time. It takes Pop a good hour to get useless drunk, even drinking on the house. But what are we dreaming about, Custis? They ain't about to let me have Indian help. If I hired Indians they'd have to let others hire Indians. Then where would Sitka be?"

"A lot more civilized. I'll bet there's dozens of housewives who could use some help with their dusting and Lord knows any Tlingit gal with a lick of ambition would rather do housework than beg at the back doors of houses."

Doris nodded and said, "I know. When we go upstairs later on, remind me to show you something."

He chuckled fondly and asked what could be left. She blushed. "Don't talk dirty, It's early yet. What I meant was a cedar-bark basket, wove so good it can hold water. The old squaw gave it to me died last winter. Afore that she used to sneak along the alley out back after dark and I'd slip her some leftovers and, well, once in a while some loose change. I know they say you ain't supposed to encourage 'em that way, but she was so old and you could tell she'd once been proud."

Longarm nodded soberly. "She must have been, to offer you handiwork of the long ago. Mission Indians don't go in much for such trades as cedar-bark weaving. It's one of the first things we try to get 'em to forget. I'd hang on to that basket, Doris. One day it may be worth something."

She shrugged. "It's just an old basket. I keep sewing

in it. But it is well made and I was sort of touched by the gift. It was funny how she gave it to me one night, just afore they said she'd died. I heard her tapping on the back door and gathered up a gunny of provisions. But when I opened the door she was standing there unusual. She'd combed her usually messy white hair and had on this fancy bark blanket, all covered with totempole faces. I offered her the provisions. But that night she wouldn't take 'em. She said she was fixing to go visit some Indian calt Raven and that she wanted me to have her basket because I was a good person. What do you reckon she meant by that, Custis?"

He swallowed and said, "She meant what she said. The basket was likely all she had left to give. They'd have buried her in that old ceremonial chilkat. Like I said, hang on to her gift. Even if it's never worth nothing, it was a gift of the heart, and you'd earned it."

Doris shrugged, picking up another glass to wipe. Then she swore and said, "Oh, damn, this ones out of service entire until I can soak the soap scum off. It could give one the trots to drink outten a glass so soapy."

Longarm nodded. "Speaking of soapy, that's the other reason I dropped by. I told a rascal called Soapy Smith to leave word here as to his present whereabouts, once he knew where he was. Has he been in yet, honey?"

She grimaced. "He has, and I said no. He said to tell you he's staying at the Widow Green's rooming house around the corner. Why do you have such disgusting friends, Custis?"

Longarm smiled crookedly. "He ain't my friend, and I agree he's disgusting. That was my other reason for dropping by a minute. You're the least disgusting friend I has in Sitka, and I never get tired of looking at you. Did he really give you a hard time? I can't shoot him just yet, but I told him to make no pass at you, and he can testify at that court-martial just as good with a busted nose than without one."

She looked pleased by his rough gallantry, but said, "Oh, he wasn't fresh enough to beat up. I hear worse all night ahint this bar. He just asked if I'd like to be kissed all over, and settled for a bar of soap."

"A bar of what?"

"Soap. Plain old kitchen soap. I gave him a brick of brown soap. He gave me the nickel I'd paid for it and went off whistling."

Longarm swore softly. "I'll see you later. The Widow Green's, you said? I *told* that son of a bitch, but he's just to dumb to listen, I reckon."

He kissed Doris and went looking for the habitual criminal he hoped was still around the corner. For once things turned out right. The Widow Green was a nice old lady so dumb she told Longarm she did indeed have a nice young gent named Smith bedded down up the stairs and that she'd be proud to show him the way. When she rapped on Soapy Smith's chamber door and the oily crook opened it, Longarm thanked her and got rid of her before he stepped inside, grabbed Smith by the front of the shirt, and said, "All right, you good-for-nothing bastard. Have you any last words before I clean your plow?"

Soapy Smith gasped. "Put me down, damn it! I ain't done nothing."

Longarm pointed at the mess on the nearby dresser drawer. "What do you call all them bitty squares of brown soap, you lying son of a bitch?"

"Fair and square. Let go my shirt and I'll show you."

Longarm let the slicker go and followed him over to the dresser. Soapy Smith picked up one of the squares of colored paper he'd cut up along with the soap and wrapped it neatly, asking, "Do you know if I just wrapped a ten-dollar bill inside this package or not, old pal?"

Longarm frowned. "I don't know if you wrapped a peso, a pound, or nothing at all. You move your hands too sneaky."

Soapy Smith wrapped another, set it aside, and said, "That time I did. I mean I really did. Go ahead and look."

Longarm picked up the wrapped soap, unwrapped it, and took out the limp ten-dollar silver certificate. As Soapy took it back, uninvited, Longarm said, "All right. So what?"

"You know my pitch. I assemble a crowd of rubes to explain how I am introducing a new line of soap at a dollar a cake."

"Soapy, that soap cost a nickel when it was all in one piece."

"Hell, Longarm, I know that and you know that. These bitty cakes are still real soap, they'll still wash duds and such. That's why I figure each cake is worth a dollar. Naturally, some rube in the crowd always asks the same smart question. I smile sort of sheepish and admit it hardly seems possible one little cake of my new soap is so valuable."

He struck a pose and in a carnival barker tone went on, "So I'll tell you what I'm going to do, ladies and gents. Just to make this interesting. Just this one time only, I am going to wrap a ten-dollar bill, as you see here, inside the package of this mighty good soap. Then we're going to mix 'em up like this, and then I'm selling each and every cake at a dollar a cake, come one come all, and please don't unwrap your own soap until you leave, lest you put me out of business premature."

Longarm said, "Soapy, you know damn well that if I

160

bought a cake of soap for a dollar, hoping to find it wrapped in a ten-dollar bill, I'd open it on the spot."

Smith grinned. "Sure you would. Everybody does and I act vexed as hell. For, as anyone can see, as the pile shrinks the odds of buying the right bar goes up. Towards the end there's ever so much pushing and shoving as the rubes try to buy that one lucky bar."

"Only there ain't bar one of soap with a ten-dollar bill wrapped around it. For you never meant anyone to buy that one, right?"

"Wrong. Do I look like a gent who looks well in tar and feathers? I always make sure someone in the crowd wins the ten dollars near the end of the pitch. Naturally, I palm said package until the rest has been nearly sold. It's untidy to hold out to the very *last* bar. Too obvious."

Longarm frowned down at the remains of the once much larger nickel bar as he muttered, "Hold on, if you really let one sucker win in the end, where's the profit in your flimflam? Seems to me. . . . Never mind. I can count. Forty slivers sold for forty dollars less ten dollars and a nickel do add up to a handsome profit. You sure cut soap small as well as neat, Soapy. But I told you I didn't want you flimflamming anyone here in Sitka before I left, and I ain't left yet."

Soapy Smith looked sincere as he asked innocently, "Hell, what's dishonest about the deal, Longarm? Nobody figures to get robbed, and one wins ten dollars of my hard-earned money every pitch."

Longarm saw that the amoral outcast really couldn't see anything wrong with his notions of selling soap. So, to save time, Longarm said, "Just don't do it while I'm still here. Like the Indian chief said, I have spoken. How come some of this paper's silvered, some green, some red, and some plain white?"

"Oh, that's just distractification. As I say I'm wrapping the money up with the soap I'm waving a sheet of silvered paper. So naturally some crook in the crowd always thinks he can cheat by buying all four silvery bars in a row. I make sure the money's in a plain white wrapper. They generally sell last, even when they ain't up my sleeve."

Longarm laughed despite himself. "You should have become a stage magician. You're good at slickery and I'm sure you're going to die younger at the rate you're going. I know how magicians try to distract you by getting you to look one way when you should be looking another, and. . . . Oh, you stupid bastard!"

Soapy Smith frowned. "I ain't a stupid bastard. I'm smart as hell."

Longarm said, "That's debatable, but I was talking about *me*. You remember them so-so valuable rubies someone asked me to hold for 'em without asking? They was the half-naked magician's assistant I was supposed to keep my eye on while the rabbit was put in the hat. The string of semi-precious was a giveaway prize nobody wanted back at all. I got distracted more when a small-time cheating wife sent a small-time pair of thugs to take 'em off me because to *small-time* crooks such a prize would be *worth* a killing!"

Soapy Smith nodded, but asked, "Then what's the real sting? It has to be for higher stakes than bare ruby legs is worth, right?"

"Yeah, and the throwaway rubies are worth at least a thousand, maybe more. Oh, shit, that one gal's looking for diamonds and diamonds are worth way more than rubies. But hold the thought. *She* sent out of her way, considerable, to attract my attention, too!"

Soapy Smith said, "Try her this way. What if someone

162

else is after the diamonds, don't know where they may be, and mean to grab her once she finds 'em? Didn't you say the rubies someone slipped in your pockets made you suspicious of *her?*"

"I got lots of good reasons to suspicion her. She's almost as big a crook as you are, Soapy. But you're right. I have been treating the poor little diamond digger surly, and she's all alone out there in the woods. I'd best go make sure she's still alive."

"Want me to come along?"

Longarm started to nod. Then he said, "No. If she needs my protection more than my arresting we might want to make up some in private."

Chapter 13

He didn't think Doris would understand. So what she might not know might not hurt her and, hell, for all he knew Tasha would be mad at him this time.

As it turned out, there was no way to know when he got to the old deserted and now sort of dug-up farm. Tasha hadn't filled in one hole. But she'd packed her possibles and lit out, unless someone had rolled up her bedding for her in the middle of a kidnapping. He doubted that. There were no signs of struggle in the deserted cabin.

He got back to town as soon as he was able. He didn't see Tasha staring in any shop windows along the main drag. So he went to the shack they used for a city hall and asked the town law if he'd noticed any Russian princesses recent.

The copper badge didn't remove his gumboots from the top of his desk as he drawled, "Sure, that Natasha woman come in a spell back in a hired rig, dressed like a man. Next time I seen the sassy thing she had her limbs hid proper in a regular she-male outfit. Had on a big fancy hat, too. I hates to see women in pants, don't you?"

"Never mind what she's wearing right now. Where's she at?"

"Don't know. Didn't ask her, so she didn't say. She likely means to catch the *Sitka Sally* out, come morning. We don't allow folk to sleep in the street out front. So she's likely bedded down in some rooming house till it's time to board the steamer."

Longarm frowned and said, "Has it been that long? I didn't know the steamer had come in yet."

"It ain't. It figures to show up around midnight, wait till the sun comes up around two, and head back to Seattle. If you don't see her afore then, that's where you'd best look for her. Is there anything else I can do for you, Longarm?"

The tall federal agent stared down poker-faced and said, "Yeah. I know you don't write the town ordinances you enforce. You don't look dumb enough. But you can pass on my message to the powers that be. I know it's considered civilized to shit on Indians, but you boys are shitting on the Tlingit more than federal law allows. When I get back to the States I mean to tell the B.I.A. they've repealed that fool law against Indians seeking work or even walking the street in some parts of this town. If they know what's good for 'em, they won't make a liar out of me."

That put the town law's feet on the floor. He frowned up to say, "Hell, Longarm, where I come from they don't allow *niggers* in the white parts of town, and some niggers can even read and write."

Longarm said, "Colored folk are at the disadvantage

166

of being U. S. citizens, since the war, at least. Indians, by federal law, which you ain't, are held to be wards of the U. S. government. So nobody but the B.I.A. Interior Department has any say about where any Indian may or may not be at a given moment. It's B.I.A. policy to encourage peacefully inclined Indians to assimilate. Reservations are more expensive to run, and even an Indian has to eat. So it ain't for you locals to say whether an honest Indian is allowed to look for a new hat or a decent job in town."

"Come on, old son, you know they're mostly thieving beggars!"

"I won't comment on why some are forced to beg or steal now that we've turned them into something as won't fit into tribal ways and ain't accepted by us after all the trouble we took teaching 'em to act more Christian. If you have a town ordinance against begging, so be it. If you catch anyone, red or white, with the wrong watch in the wrong pocket, you can still arrest 'em. But nobody can arrest an Indian just for being an Indian without Uncle Sam's permission, and it wouldn't be smart to ask him. So far, you civilians up here have had it mighty easy under a lax military government. Stir up enough interest for Washington to send up a fully staffed B.I.A. agency and, for openers, they'll start by pressing federal charges against every old boy in town who's ever laid a Tlingit gal or given her father a bottle. The wilder Tlingit out in the trees are more pissed off at you than I am, and I mean to have a word with the navy about their complaints before I go. So I'll only say this, and you'd best pass it around. Katchatag is armed and dangerous and has you whites out-numbered more than ten to one. If you keep ignoring his just gripes, he'll likely rise again you. He'll lose, of course. But a lot of you will die in the meanwhile.

The survivors will have B.I.A. agents watching every time they want to go fishing or cut firewood. I don't know why they failed to put it in the Good Book more, but there's more to treating folk decent than a pat on the halo in the sweet by and by. Treating folk right can be *smart* as well as decent."

The town law assured him he'd pass on the message. Longarm left. He didn't go looking for Tasha. He didn't know where to begin, and he had other fish to fry. He stopped at the telegraph office on the way to the naval base and had another heated discussion in the officers' club. Once they had that settled, he went back to the saloon to await further developments.

It was crowded now, and Doris was working fit to bust. He didn't think the Department would approve of a federal agent working as a barkeep, so he picked up a rack of really disgusting glasses and took them out back to rinse.

He ran lots of water in the big tin sink and added some vinegar to it. Then he hung up his hat and coat, rolled up his sleeves, and got to work. The vinegar seemed to be cutting the soap scum pretty good. He had half the glassware clean when he heard a timid tapping on the back door, dried his hands on a towel, and went to answer it.

Tasha popped in, sort of breathless, to gasp, "I didn't want anyone to see us together, even if I was up to entering a saloon by the front way. Is it safe to talk in here, darling?"

Longarm said, "Sure, that gal staring at us from yonder calendar is good at keeping secrets. What secrets are we talking about, Tasha?"

"I found them. Just this afternoon. As I was packing

to leave, I was sure someone was watching me from the woods!"

"I told you the Indians would be. Let's see the stones you dug out of all them rocks."

She followed him over to the light above the sink as she handed him a rusty tin box. He opened it and said, "Oops!" as the pint or more of fire and ice spilled over some and three or four stones plopped into the rinse water.

Tasha gasped, "You fool!"

"Simmer down," he soothed. "They ain't going no-where, unless I pull the stopper."

He placed the box of diamonds on the drainboard and reached both hands down to feel for them along the shiny bottom. He found the first one and placed it on the drain-board to dry. He tested the second one against a beer glass before he removed both the glass and the cut stone from the water. Tasha didn't notice how he'd cut an X in the glass with her diamond to test it. She wasn't sup-posed to. That was why Longarm had spilled the gems in the sink in the first place.

It was a little tougher to find the others. So he took the word of the beer glass on the one and got them all back in the box for Tasha, saying, "Well, if them's real diamonds, you have to have over a million dollars worth. What am *I* supposed to do about it? I don't think I'm likely to make enough to buy one of 'em for quite a spell."

"Now that I've found them at last I'm scared skinny of *losing* them! Would you hold them for me until we can board the steamer in the morning and I can store them in the purser's safe?"

He frowned down at her. "I was sure I told you I

wasn't free to leave here until they held that court-martial, Tasha. Lord knows when that might be at the rate they're going."

She pouted. "Damn, I was looking forward to the other pleasures of your company on the way south, too. But couldn't you at least see me off? If you put me and these diamonds safely aboard, nobody could rob me along the way, and I could wire someone to meet me in Seattle with a gun."

He nodded. "We got a safe out front. I'll ask my pal Doris to let us use it. Come, say, midnight, you just get up and meet me on the dock. We'll go right aboard, I'll turn the box over to the purser, and that'll be that. Wire your gunslinger in Seattle before you board the steamer, of course."

She leaned closer and said, "I knew I could count on you, darling. Why don't I just wait here while you put the gems in the saloon safe? Then we can go back to my place and wait together until we have to say goodbye."

He shook his head and said, "We got to be practical, honey. Doris is a sport, up to a point. But how many gals would let another gal use their safe free, and then borrow their dishwasher as well?"

"Oh, is that the way things stand between you and that cheap little barmaid, Custis?"

"Don't talk spiteful about a lady who's doing you a favor. If you don't like the deal, go find another free bodyguard. I still got some glassware to do here."

She sighed. "Oh, hell, try to save some for me. The boat may not be leaving right away." Then she gave him a sisterly kiss and went out the way she'd come in. Longarm dried his hands and went to join Doris behind the bar. He gave her the box and said, "I'd like to keep this in your safe a spell. Don't open it in front of God

170

and everybody. I'll show you what's inside, later."

She said she would and asked if he was going out again. He said he might be, but that he'd be back before midnight because he had to be. Doris looked at the wall clock and leaned closer to say, "Don't take that long. Pop just came in, sober, and I mean to turn the bar over to him so we can turn in early. Jesus, I'm hot for you right now!"

He sighed, went back to the kitchen with another tray of glasses, and rinsed them clean. Then he ducked out the back to go to the Western Union and wire Billy Vail about some changes in plans he was still working on. He told the clerk to send them direct and to wake Vail up in Denver if need be; he would come back for the answer in a little while.

Longarm walked the length of the main drag to stretch his legs, gather his wits, and make sure Soapy Smith was behaving himself. The street was crowded because the steamboat was due to arrive. But nothing too interesting happened, even though he was hoping something might.

He went back to the saloon. Doris must have been listening for her back door to open even though someone was playing the piano out front. For she joined him, looking expectant, and said, "I'm free now. Unless you want me to screw you on that butcher's block, we'd better get upstairs."

They did, and Doris must have meant it, for she screwed him silly. When they came back down from heaven Longarm got out his watch as well as the usual cheroot and matches. He sighed and said, "I got to leave soon, Doris. Would you do me a favor? Would you put them rubies on for me again?"

She giggled and rolled naked out of bed to do so. As

she stood by candlelight, the red gems glistening against her smooth naked skin, she asked him how she looked. He said, "You look grand, and I'll always remember you that way, little darling. They're yours."

Doris gasped, clutching the rubies to her naked breasts. "Don't fun me, Custis! You know I'd give my heart and soul for anything so lovely, but—"

"You already did," he cut in, "so we'll say no more about it. I would have given 'em to you sooner, knowing how you admired 'em, and how pretty they looked on you. But until recent, I thought they was evidence. Now they ain't. So consider 'em my cedar basket to a decent human being."

She started to cry, asking how he could afford such a treasure for a gal like her. He thought she was a good old gal and it made him feel sort of cheap, when he considered what he'd paid for a gift that meant so much to her. "Don't blubber up on me," he told her. "Slip something on so's we can get them diamonds from the safe."

"My God, is that what's in that box, diamonds?"

"Yeah. I'm sorry, but you can't have *them*. Where did I leave my fool pants? You sure undress a man passionate, Doris."

He found his duds here and there on the floor and got dressed as Doris, for some fool reason, put her best low-cut dress on, still wearing her new red play-pretties. She admired herself in the mirror as he rose from the edge of the bed.

They went down to get Tasha's box from the safe. As she handed it to him, Doris said, "Don't show me, Custis. For if there are prettier jewels in the whole wide world than the ones you just gave me, I never want to see 'em."

He kissed her goodbye in the kitchen, pocketed the

box, and went back to the Western Union. The clerk said no to all his questions. Longarm sighed and headed for the steamer dock. Sometimes a field agent just had to think for himself, no matter what the regulations might say.

Chapter 14

The *Sitka Sally* had put in and there were lots of townees on the dock to stare at her in the late-night sunshine. Tasha wasn't alone on the dock as she paced it nervously. When she spied Longarm she ran up to him and gasped, "I was starting to worry. I knew you were a lawman, but every man has his price."

He said, "I'm paid a mite better than your average cowhand. Let's get aboard with these rocks."

They did, and scouted up the ship's purser. He said he would be proud to put Tasha's treasure trove under lock and key, but insisted on looking at the contents in his own cubbyhole. He made Longarm as well as Tasha sign a receipt for the diamonds after he had counted every damned one, and there were over a hundred.

Out in the companionway, Tasha turned to Longarm. "I feel ever so much better, now. I hope you don't have to leave right away, darling."

Longarm said he had plenty of time. She brought him to her stateroom, dragged his duds off, and said she could see he'd saved some for her after all.

He had, guessing in advance that Tasha would want to get sassy. He found his new surroundings gave him new inspiration as well. They were going at it hot and heavy when they heard the warning whistle sound and Tasha said, "Oh, damn. You have to get off. The boat, I mean."

Longarm just kept doing what he liked to do best as he assured her, "There's no need to hurry. We got this whole night and more ahead of us before we reach Seattle."

She stopped moving her hips in time with his thrusts. "Oh? I thought you said you had to stay for the court-martial of that naval deserter, dear."

"I lied. I don't show my cards any more than I have to, in a game of poker or on duty. The navy has an air-tight case with Soapy Smith in the flesh willing to testify he's the one in the witness chair, not the one in the brig. So I told 'em I had to head home, and they didn't argue. Could you move a little, honey? No offense, but it ain't much fun when a gal just lies there like a side of beef."

Tasha wrapped her legs around his hips and started moving like the experienced woman of the world she was. But she sounded more curious than passionate as she asked him, "Why did you have to lie to *me* of all people? Surely you don't suspect me of anything now?"

"I don't suspect nothing. I got it all figured out and— Powder River if I ain't coming, you sweet thing!"

She asked him, cool and innocent, "Just what are you trying to tell me, Custis? Is this a screwing or an arrest we're discussing, you brute?"

He relaxed atop her. "Hell, we both know I can't arrest you. Your lawyers would make hash out of my testimony in court unless I perjured myself about screwing you just now, and I hate to lie in court."

She started moving under him, teasingly, the way worried women tended to when captured by Indians or in the arms of the law. He enjoyed it. Tasha was an even better lay than she was a crook. She faked an orgasm, accepted another real one from him, and sighed, "Oh, that felt lovely, dear. For a minute there I thought you were mad at me."

He said, "I ain't mad at nobody. Just doing my job. The diamonds you stole are in the safe. The arresting officers will be waiting for you on the Seattle dock. So I see no need for us to act like strangers before we get there, do you?"

She gasped. "You're crazy! Nobody can arrest *me!* I haven't done anything wrong!" She giggled weakly and hugged him tighter. "Except *this,* of course, and you just said you'd never want to tell a judge and jury how naughty I can get when I'm feeling passionate."

He laughed coldly, despite the warm way he was moving in her again. "You're about as passionate as a snowbank, but a lot more pretty, and cool can be a refreshing change, when it's free."

"You bastard! Get off me! Unless you want to be nice and tell me what this is all about."

"Hell, didn't you know? You was the one set it up, from start to finish. You've admitted you was the mistress of an old established dealer in stolen property. The Seattle police admitted they found the pickings slim when they finally got a court order to look through his safe when he passed away. They didn't find the fortune in diamonds and some lesser gem stones, because you'd already helped yourself to 'em."

"Custis, that's just not true! I told you he'd left the diamonds in Alaska when he had to flee the Russian police. You saw me dig them up on his old family farm, damn it!"

He laughed and said, "No, I never. You let me and the Indians witness you digging all over, on a farm Rostov never owned, in gravel dirt, with a miner's pick. A total moron might not have known better than to swing a pick anywheres near a thin tin box full of brittle diamonds. But you did time for jewel theft, and you lived with a dealer in stolen jewels. You never swung no pick at them diamonds in the purser's safe. You had 'em on you all the time, meaning to do what you just tried to do: dig 'em up innocent and claim 'em as a lawful treasure trove, with the purser and me as witnesses they come from Alaska instead of the ladies who lost 'em in less wild parts. Then you meant to sell 'em on the open market, as long-lost Russian jewels instead of hot ice some rightful owners are no doubt still weeping over."

She tried to brazen it out by insisting, "So you say. Maybe I *was* in a careless hurry to dig them up, with those Indians skulking about and all. But how could I have had stolen property on me when I went through Customs with you on arrival? You saw them search me, Custis."

He nuzzled her ear and said, "Yeah. You didn't know beans about Alaska, never having been there before. So you went to more trouble than you needed to, smuggling the diamonds in. You hid 'em in plain sight, in them bottles of clear Russian vodka, knowing diamonds are

178

invisible in water or any other clear liquid. But you was still a mite nervous, being a professional thief instead of a professional smuggler. So to give yourself a further edge, you planted them rubies on me, hoping that if the Customs search was thorough a man you knew as the law would raise so much hell about being accused of smuggling that nobody would notice little innocent you in the crowd.

"I confess them rubies confused me a lot more than they did the naval officers who just went through the motions. We both know they wasn't worth much to a gal with a million or more in diamonds. That's how you could afford to give 'em away and refuse to have 'em back. Greedier folk took 'em more serious and muddied the waters for you even more than you'd intended. But as I told you the time you hung from the coat rack, you're a gal who takes her opportunities where she finds 'em. Knowing I was stuck in Sitka, or thinking you knew I was, you tried to use me some more. That's all right. I *enjoy* the way you use men."

He was enjoying the game more than he was enjoying her flesh. "You dropped the Russian princess act, once you knew I'd had time to find out who you really were, even though I hadn't, yet. You only acted Russian in the first place as an excuse to unload all that vodka. The wine and Canadian redeye a French Canuck like you would be more apt to drink wouldn't have worked as well, iced with clear diamonds. You did what you could to stay on the best side of me, letting me think I was slickering you. Then you tried to slicker me by asking me to guard the diamonds you'd just dug up like spuds and sign them aboard this vessel for you. We know how *that* just turned out."

"You . . . dirty . . . sneaky . . . bastard! Get off, and don't you ever touch me again!"

He rolled off and sat up to grope for a smoke. "Takes one to know one, I reckon. This sure figures to be a tedious trip if you aim to be so *surly* about it. You know, of course, it may be some time before you'll get a chance to get laid again, once this ship docks. I can't arrest you. So I don't see why we can't still be pals."

As he lit a cheroot she sat up, covering her breasts with her hands for some reason, and said in a small, sad voice, "That's all too true! You'll be the last man who's ever touched me that way. For I'll never be sent back to that prison again! They could give me twenty years!"

He nodded. "At *least* twenty, seeing as it ain't the first time for you. I'm sorry about that, Tasha, for you really are a pretty little gal, and I was hoping all along you was innocent."

She rose from the rumpled bed. He saw no need to stop her, as long as he kept an eye on his guns. But when she opened the outside door to the dark deck, he frowned and asked, "Where in the hell do you think you're going at this hour in your birthday suit, girl? I'll leave if my company upsets you so. There ain't no place for you to run or hide. So get back in here before you shock more proper passengers, damn it!"

She didn't answer. She just stepped out on deck, naked as a jay, and before Longarm could stop her she was over the side and under the paddlewheel.

Longarm started down over the rail as the cold sea breeze chilled his naked skin. Then he ducked back inside, slammed the door, and sat down weakly, muttering, "I wish folk wouldn't do that."

He got dressed and went up to the bridge to report a

woman overboard, cleaning the matter up as much as he could without lying. From the way the ship's watch commander took it one might have thought they were talking about his own daughter, even though he did agree there was no use putting about to search in the dark for what that big side paddle might have left of Tasha in the ice-cold water.

He said, "The company's going to have a fit over this. But I don't suppose there's any way to hush up a federal case, cuss her impulsive nature!"

Longarm lit a cheroot before he replied. "It ain't federal. I was never sent up this way on her case. She dragged me in. I told her it was up to the Seattle police to arrest her and recover the jewels from your purser's safe. But nobody ever listens."

"You mean Uncle Sam won't raise an eyebrow if the steamship line and Seattle agree on a less shocking news release than a bare-ass midnight swim under flashing paddle blades?"

Longarm shrugged. "It won'd do nobody no good to brag about her one way or the other, now. The gals the stones belong to by law will be happy to get 'em back. The gal who meant to keep 'em may be happier dead than in prison. You and the local law can settle the matter between you any way you want. As of now, I'm off the case."

He blew a thoughtful smoke ring and added, "I wish I was off this vessel as well. From here on, this voyage promises to get tedious as hell."

Longarm went down to his own less fancy stateroom facing inward on the companionway and got a good night's sleep as the sun came up again. Then he rose, long after his watch said he should be getting cussed by Billy Vail for showing up for work so late, and found they were still serving breakfast. He enjoyed a good one, went aft to the main salon, and sat down to enjoy the passing scenery of the Inland Passage. Just as he was getting tired of gazing on misty spruce-covered hills, a woman's voice asked him if he knew what all the fuss the night before had been about. Longarm turned to gaze on her scenery and saw she had red hair, green eyes, and a cute little turned-up nose. He took off his Stetson, laid it aside, and said, "I ain't sure, ma'am. But maybe if we put our heads together we can figure something out."

Watch for

LONGARM IN THE RUBY RANGE COUNTRY

ninetieth novel in the bold
LONGARM series from Jove

coming in June!

Explore the exciting Old West with
one of the men who made it wild!

___08551-0	**LONGARM #1**	$2.50
___07067-X	**LONGARM ON THE BIG MUDDY #29**	$2.50
___06582-X	**LONGARM AND THE GOLDEN LADY #32**	$2.50
___07414-4	**LONGARM IN THE BIG THICKET #48**	$2.50
___07522-1	**LONGARM AND THE EASTERN DUDES #49**	$2.50
___07854-9	**LONGARM IN THE BIG BEND #50**	$2.50
___07722-4	**LONGARM ON THE GREAT DIVIDE #52**	$2.50
___08101-9	**LONGARM AND THE BUCKSKIN ROGUE #53**	$2.50
___08099-3	**LONGARM AND THE OUTLAW LAWMAN #56**	$2.50
___07859-X	**LONGARM AND THE BOUNTY HUNTERS #57**	$2.50
___07858-1	**LONGARM IN NO MAN'S LAND #58**	$2.50
___07886-7	**LONGARM AND THE BIG OUTFIT #59**	$2.50
___08259-7	**LONGARM AND SANTA ANNA'S GOLD #60**	$2.50
___08388-7	**LONGARM AND THE CUSTER COUNTY WAR #61**	$2.50
___08161-2	**LONGARM IN VIRGINIA CITY #62**	$2.50

Prices may be slightly higher in Canada.

Available at your local bookstore or return this form to:

 JOVE
THE BERKLEY PUBLISHING GROUP, Dept. B
390 Murray Hill Parkway, East Rutherford, NJ 07073

Please send me the titles checked above. I enclose _____ Include $1.00 for postage and handling if one book is ordered; 25¢ per book for two or more not to exceed $1.75. California, Illinois, New Jersey and Tennessee residents please add sales tax. Prices subject to change without notice and may be higher in Canada.

NAME_____

ADDRESS_____

CITY_____STATE/ZIP_____

(Allow six weeks for delivery.)

5